Journey Through the Impossible

Journey Through the Impossible

by

Jules Verne

TRANSLATED BY Edward Baxter

INTRODUCTION BY Jean-Michel Margot
President, North American Jules Verne Society

ORIGINAL ARTWORK BY Roger Leyonmark

Prometheus Books
59 John Glenn Drive
Amherst, New York 14228-2197

Published 2003 by Prometheus Books

Inquiries should be addressed to
Prometheus Books
59 John Glenn Drive
Amherst, New York 14228–2197
VOICE: 716–691–0133, ext. 207
FAX: 716–564–2711
WWW.PROMETHEUSBOOKS.COM

07 06 05 04 03   5 4 3 2 1

Library of Congress Cataloging-in-Publication Data

Verne, Jules, 1828–1905.
  [Voyage à travers l'impossible. English]
  Journey through the impossible / by Jules Verne ; translated by Edward Baxter.
    p. cm.
  ISBN 1–59102–079–4 (cloth : alk. paper)
  I. Baxter, Edward. II. Title.
PQ2469.V7313 2003
843'8—dc21

                                                      2003004668

Printed in Canada on acid-free paper

Contents

Acknowledgments   9

Introduction by Jean-Michel Margot
          President, North American Jules Verne Society   11

Synopsis of the Play   21

Cast of Characters   25

ACT I: THE CENTER OF THE EARTH

Scene 1: Andernak Castle   33

Scene 2: The Fallen Angel   47

Scene 3: The Inn　　　　　　　　　　　49

Scene 4: Five Hundred Leagues Underground　　60

Scene 5: The Central Fire　　　　　　　　70

ACT II: THE BOTTOM OF THE SEA

Scene 1: The Harbor at Goa　　　　　　　75

Scene 2: The Platform of the *Nautilus*　　　84

Scene 3: The *Nautilus*　　　　　　　　86

Scene 4: Underwater Navigation　　　　　90

Scene 5: On the Ocean Floor　　　　　　90

Scene 6: An Underwater Forest　　　　　91

Scene 7: The Coral Reef　　　　　　　94

Scene 8: Atlantis　　　　　　　　　　96

ACT III: THE PLANET ALTOR

Scene 1: The Gun Club　　　　　　　109

Scene 2: The Cannon Shot　　　　　　119

Scene 3: The Planet Altor　　　　　　125

Scene 4: The End of a World　　　　　138

Scene 5: The Explosion　　　　　　　140

Scene 6: Andernak Castle   140

Scene 7: Apotheosis   143

Appendices: 1882: Two Reviews of
           Journey Through the Impossible   145

           Arnold Mortier: Evenings in Paris in 1882
           (November 25)   147

           The New York Times
           "A Jules Verne Piece"
           (December 19)   155

Notes   161

Acknowledgments

With the publication of *Journey Through the Impossible* a dream comes true. The North American Jules Verne Society (NAJVS) presents to the English-speaking world this heretofore unpublished play. This edition is the result of a collaboration between several members of the NAJVS and their friends. Edward Baxter translated the text from the original French and it is his translation we publish here. Two other translators independently rendered the play into English: Cecile Molla Leyonmark and Frank Morlock. Cecile's translation was published in *Extraordinary Voyages*, the NAJVS newsletter. Frank is a professional translator of Dumas' plays and he enjoys translating Verne's plays. His Dumas translations are available at www.roguepublishing.com/.

Edward Baxter has already translated several of Verne's works,[1] and we hope he will for many years continue to help "rescue" these works, so that Verne will be recognized in America, finally, as a writer and stylist. Our thanks go also to the board of directors of the NAJVS, chaired by Dennis Kytasaari until June 2002, and to the members of the Translations Committee: Walter James Miller, Brian Taves, and Roger Leyonmark. The elegant illustrations created by Roger Leyonmark and which adorn the cover, the frontispiece, and serve to open each act of the present play, help the reader travel to the center of the earth, through oceans, and to the planet Altor.

We are also grateful to Anna Jean Mayhew, a professional editor and one of the newest members of NAJVS, for her careful attention to this introduction and to the notes throughout the play.

Three prominent members of the French Société Jules Verne helped us tremendously with first-hand information: Robert Pourvoyeur, the world specialist of Offenbach and of Verne's plays; the late François Raymond (d. 1993), who edited the French edition of the play; and Volker Dehs, whose curiosity and tenacity make him the "Vernian detective." Steven L. Mitchell, our editor at Prometheus Books, brings this unknown and unexpected Verne play to life in America.

Introduction

BY

JEAN-MICHEL MARGOT

*J*ourney Through the Impossible (*Voyage à travers l'impossible*) is for many readers an unexpected and surprising work by the French novelist Jules Verne (1828–1905). First, the piece is a play and not a novel. Second, when staged in Paris in 1882, the play included "special effects," as they are called today. Third, Verne took characters from his former novels and short stories (like Captain Nemo of *Twenty Thousand Leagues Under the Sea*[1] and Michel Ardan of *From the Earth to the Moon*[2]), resurrecting them for great adventures in *Journey Through the Impossible*. Fourth, the play was written in the middle of Verne's life, between his optimistic and pessimistic periods. Fifth, of all Verne's work, this is the one most oriented toward science fiction; the play includes travel to the interior of the earth, under the oceans, and into outer space. Sixth, for almost a century the piece was lost to Vernian scholars. Seventh, the play was never translated and the publisher of the original French edition overlooked a scene. The omitted scene is included in this first complete edition of *Journey Through the Impossible*.

Verne, known in the United States as "the father of science fiction," wrote mainly geographic and scientific adventure novels between 1862 and 1905.[3] These works were published in Paris by Pierre-Jules Hetzel,[4] his lifelong publisher. In his novels, only on exceptional occasions does Verne step out of what is possible, what can be scientifically explained; for the most part he stays in the real world. For example, Verne's *The Sphinx of the Ice*[5] and H. P. Lovecraft's *At the Mountains of Madness*,[6] are both sequels to the unfinished *Adventures of Arthur Gordon Pym*[7] by Edgar Allen Poe. However, Verne explains rationally the supernatural apparition that comes out of the fog in the last pages of Poe's book. Lovecraft does not unveil the mystery, and even enhances it.

Silence surrounded a work whose title suggested a fundamental departure from all his other work, and whose goal was to go beyond the limits of the *Extraordinary Voyages*.[8] In 1904, when interviewed by the British journalist Gordon Jones,[9] Verne said, "But these results are merely the natural outcome of the scientific trend of modern thought, and as such have doubtless been predicted by scores of others besides myself. Their coming was inevitable, whether anticipated or not, and the most that I can claim is to have looked perhaps a little farther into the future than the majority of my critics." And yet here is *Voyage Through the Impossible*, a play in three acts, written with d'Ennery[10] and performed over two decades earlier; the play is in complete contradiction to the above affirmation!

Before becoming well known in 1863 upon publication of *Five Weeks in a Balloon*,[11] Verne wrote numerous plays (most are not yet translated into English), and many of his novels are structured like plays, using the "coup de théâtre" to refresh the reader's attention. Three novels—*Around the World in Eighty Days*,[12] *Michael Strogoff*,[13] and *The Children of Captain Grant*[14] (also known as *In Search of the Castaways*)—were rewritten as plays and published as a book in 1881 by Hetzel under the title *The Journeys on Stage*.[15] They were performed for several years in Paris and their huge success made Verne wealthy.

The plays became grand spectacles, due to the genius of d'Ennery, who brought to the stage an elephant, water fountains, and Indians chasing a train. Without movies and television, the people of Paris went to the theatre, and the name *pièce à grand spectacle* (extravaganza) is reserved for plays of the second half of the nineteenth century with huge, colorful, animated sets. The success of these plays was such that some were brought to America in the 1870s and 1880s by the brothers Bolossy and Imre Kiralfy.[16] D'Ennery helped make *Journey Through the Impossible* into a *pièce à grand spectacle*—a guarantee of success. *Journey Through the Impossible* played for the first time in Paris, at the Théâtre de la Porte Saint-Martin on November 25, 1882. The play was performed 97 times (43 in 1882 and 54 in 1883), which compares well with the 113 performances of *The Children of Captain Grant*.

By 1882, Jules Verne was a world-renowned writer, thanks to a new genre, the scientific novel. His plays, a goldmine for theatre directors around the world, dramatized some of his novels, fulfilling for him a dream of his youth—to be appreciated as a playwright. In fact, young Verne, from the time of his law studies, dreamt of nothing but the theater. He was introduced into the social circles of Alexandre Dumas père,[17] and managed to have an act performed at the Théâtre Historique[18] in 1850: *The Broken Straws*.[19] He loved music, mainly opera, and in 1853 he became secretary of the Théâtre Lyrique,[20] where the most famous French operas of the nineteenth century were created under the signature of Hector Berlioz,[21] Charles-François Gounod,[22] Georges Bizet,[23] Adolphe-Charles Adam,[24] and others. Before finding his way to the publisher Hetzel and embarking on his monumental work, *Extraordinary Voyages*, Verne had written several plays, and even after starting his adventure novels, he continued to produce dramas.

But a profound change in the public's taste made Verne seek a new approach. The festive atmosphere of the Second Empire was brutally wiped away by the Franco-Prussian War of 1870, by the defeat of France, and by the bloody reprisals following the Paris Commune. In the field of theater, these events transformed theater-goers, who no longer wanted sarcastic *opéra-bouffe*,[25] loaded with verve and presupposing a wide culture among spectators who understood a world of fairies and genies. Rather, the Parisian public sought consolation and relief from a grim reality by fleeing into the world of dreams. That meant a return to a simpler form of the old *opéra-comique*,[26] a fantasy.

The Parisians wanted amazing spectacles with astonishing machines; certainly Verne's novels could be transformed into wondrous dramas with exotic sets and costumes. The success was striking and fabulous: *Around the World in Eighty Days*—a lavish production with Indians, Hindus, elephants, serpents, trains, and shipwrecks—ran for 415 successive performances from November 7, 1874 to December 20, 1875. Encouraged by this success, Verne reissued *Children of Captain Grant* in 1878 and *Michael Strogoff* in 1880.

All of these plays were in collaboration with d'Ennery, one of the most prolific drama writers of the nineteenth century. From 1831 to 1887, he presented an enormous number of plays, fantasies, libretti for opera, and other staged performances. At the time of his collaboration with Verne, d'Ennery was at the peak of his fame; he had already written his famous work, *The Two Orphans*.[27] He owned a superb villa in Antibes (on the French Riviera), a dream of a place where Verne went to work several times. (Without the help of the "special effects" magician d'Ennery, Verne later wrote two other plays inspired by his novels—*Keraban the Inflexible*[28] and *Mathias Sandorf*[29]—but they were performed only a few times.)

Verne had long pondered the dangers of science. After publication of "Master Zacharius"[30] (1854), he seemed to be influenced by Saint-Simonianism,[31] a philosophy the Second Empire tacitly adopted, that glorified the engineers, science, and technology that would industrialize France. Furthermore, in no other work by Verne are science fiction and science fantasy so present as in *Journey Through the Impossible* (1882). With regard to science fiction, even *Twenty Thousand Leagues under the Sea* and *From the Earth to the Moon* cannot compete.

Most of Jules Verne's novels until the mid-1880s present science and technology as beneficial to humankind. The scientist uses technology to help heroes out of a difficult situation. Typically, the engineer Cyrus Smith (*Mysterious Island*[32]) drives his companion castaways toward a better life, using his knowledge of chemistry, physics, and natural sciences, restructuring nature with the overriding ingenuity of humans. In Verne's novels of the first part of his life the only villain is Herr Doktor Schultze (*The Five Hundred Million of the Begum*[33]), but the character is not Verne's invention. Hetzel bought the manuscript from Paschal Grousset[34] (better known by his pseudonym, André Laurie) and asked Verne to rewrite it; the book was published as authored by Jules Verne. After the mid-1880s, Verne, in his pessimism, created crazy scientists like Robur (*Robur the Conqueror* or *Master of the World*[35]), Orfanik (*The Castle in the Carpathians*[36]), and Thomas Roch (*Facing the Flag*[37]). These mad scientists use their knowledge and inventions for destructive purposes. *Journey Through the Impossible* is the hinge between the two halves of Verne's life, being an apotheosis of the first optimistic part, where the play asks the reader and the spectator, continuously, to choose, like George Hatteras, between good and evil, heaven and hell.

From 1872, with "The Doctor Ox,"[38] Verne emphasized the danger of too much science, believing that science itself is not to blame; rather, we must look to the use humans make of science. In this short story—a vigorous and compact masterpiece of droll humor and sarcastic farce—a scientist risks a terribly dangerous experiment, even more disquieting because he pretends to provide free gas lighting for the town of Quiquendone, without charging for his scientific knowledge. The tone remains that of the opéra-bouffe of the Second Empire; thus, it comes as no surprise that the subject attracted Offenbach[39] in 1877. Peaceful, soft characters engulfed in their own bovine passivity are the foil to the bizarre and mysterious figure of Dr. Ox. No one knows where he comes from or who he is. He calls himself a doctor; he is not a professor like Lidenbrock in *Journey to the Center of the Earth*,[40] Aronnax in *Twenty Thousand Leagues under the Sea*, or Palmyrin Rosette in *Hector Servadac*.[41] Professors are reassuringly familiar by virtue of their daily contact with the students they help mold; a doctor is a far more independent and unaccountable being. Dr. Ox is unsettling, like a new incarnation of the evil who haunts *The Tales of Hoffmann*, the drama by Jules Barbier[42] and Michel Carré,[43] presented at l'Odéon[44] in 1851 (the opera by Offenbach had not yet been written). In the same year, Verne collaborated with Carré to produce a play, *Leonardo da Vinci*, which later became *Mona Lisa*,[45] with a similar underlying theme as in *The Tales of Hoffmann*—the necessity of choosing between art and love. Jules Verne said of Dr. Ox that he "escaped from a volume by Hoffmann." By Hoffmann? Or by Barbier and Carré? Or by Offenbach—his demonic and deadly Dr. Miracle? Offenbach's opera was created in Paris, February 10, 1881. The direct line from *The Tales of Hoffmann* to *Journey Through the Impossible* is obvious; Offenbach's opera has five acts: prologue, first love, second love, third love, and epilogue. In Verne's play, Act I includes the prologue and the first exploration; Act II is the second exploration, and Act III is the third exploration and the epilogue. Thus we have Hoffmann's first love (Olympia, a mechanical doll) and George Hatteras's first exploration (to the center of the earth); Hoffmann's second love (Antonia, who dies while singing) and George's second exploration (under the oceans); Hoffmann's third love (Giulietta, who steals his shadow) and George's third exploration (to outer space). Both pieces end by highlighting the battle between good and evil, with the same choice for the hero—in *Hoffmann*, between art and love; in *Journey Through the Impossible*, between science and love.

Most of the characters of *Journey Through the Impossible* were already known to the spectators. The hero, George Hatteras, is the son of Captain Hatteras, who discovered the North Pole in *Journey and Adventures of Captain Hatteras*.[46] Like the Verne novels, this play is a typical initiatory journey where George Hatteras discovers the center of the Earth, the underwater world, and the planet Altor. The journey is strenuous; George, faced with obstacles and difficulties, is subjected to evil forces that push him to journey farther, and to good forces that protect him from danger and keep him from the blasphemy of seeking to become godlike. The evil force is personified by Doctor Ox ("Doctor Ox"), without his colleague Ygène. The beneficent spirit, Volsius, first takes the identity of Otto Lidenbrock (*Journey to the Center of the Earth*), then of Captain Nemo (*Twenty Thousand Leagues under the Sea*), and, at the end, of Michel Ardan (*From the Earth to the Moon* and *Around the Moon*[47]). Volsius tries to restrain George Hatteras from his journey, but Ox coerces the hero to conquer Earth in Act I, the seas in Act II, and space in Act III. George is accompanied in his travels by Eva, his fiancée (the love interest so important to Hollywood). For comic relief, Verne and d'Ennery added Tartelet, a teacher of dance and etiquette (based on Professor T. Artelet of *The School of Robinsons*,[48] also known as *Godfrey Morgan*).

Tartelet (French for small tart) did not need time travel to jump from the novel into the play, since the former was published and the latter performed in 1882. *The School of Robinsons* was serialized from January to December 1882 in Hetzel's magazine for the French family, *Magasin d'Education et de Récréation*, and was made available as an illustrated book November 9, 1882, two weeks before *Journey Through the Impossible* was first performed in Paris. With his friend Valdemar, Tartelet teaches good manners to George and Eva throughout the play, during travels to the center of the earth, to Atlantis, and to Altor—talents very useful in such circumstances! To help the heroes get to Altor, Verne resurrected Impey Barbicane and J. T. Maston, president and secretary, respectively, of the Gun Club in Baltimore, which launched the bullet *From the Earth to the Moon* in 1865. However, the characters never reached the Moon. Likewise, having set his foot on the North Pole, Hatteras finds only emptiness, because the exact geographic pole is in the center of a volcano. The *Journey to the Center of the Earth* does not fulfill its goal, and Nemo, *Under the Sea*, does not visit the deepest abyss on the floor of the ocean. Verne's astronauts are confined to circle the Moon on their voyage *Around the Moon*. The cannon paid for with *The Five Hundred Million of the Begum* does not destroy France-Ville, and the lovers don't see *The Green Ray*.[49] At the end of his tour *Around the World in Eighty Days*,[50] Fogg does win his wager, but only by way of another typically Vernian glitch. *Michael Strogoff* arrives too late at Irkutsk, and *The Star of the South*[51] is not a synthetic diamond. We see Maston failing *Topsy-Turvy*,[52] as does *Robur the Conqueror*,[53] as do the engineers of *Propeller Island*,[54] and Orfanik's inventions for *The Castle in the Carpathians* are all destroyed. In most of the novels, however extraordinary the voyage, a reader might come to feel as if an angel with a flaming sword had risen before the writer and called out to him, "No farther! Ahead is the unknown, forbidden to humans—the realm of the impossible." After "Master Zacharius," Verne almost stopped writing fantasy and horror stories, a domain that would later occupy writers such as H. G. Wells, H. P. Lovecraft, Ray Sloane, and many others.

Nevertheless, to such a forbidden realm we are taken by the hero of *Journey Through the Impossible*, by way of the madness inherited from his father. The other characters created by Verne move through the extraordinary world of scientific realities. George Hatteras wishes to go beyond. "This is simply the extraordinary, not the impossible," he exclaims to himself. Verne does not reject characters previously created in his novels; they are, moreover, incarnations of the good— even Nemo, the rebellious anarchist, the pirate who destroys innocent vessels. This play doesn't contradict previous works; rather, it is an extension of them, setting forth the limits beyond which lie the unknowable and the inaccessible. This flamboyant subject, paradoxically, is quite modern in its "fantasy" concepts, rather than futuristic science fiction, even though the reader is distracted repeatedly by breaks in the tone or tension of the action by the goings-on of two comic characters—a Shakespearean effect that also influenced the comic interludes of Neapolitan opéra-bouffe. Constructed like a signpost at the border between the possible and the impossible, this play is, more than any other of the novelist's manuscripts, required reading for all of those, in ever-growing numbers, who study him. Verne's works are now classics in world literature, and he is a subject so complex as to be understood only from a multi-disciplinary approach.

Verne wrote two trilogies; the first includes *The Children of Captain Grant, Twenty Thousand Leagues under the Sea*, and *Mysterious Island*; the second comprises *From the Earth to the Moon, Around the Moon*, and *Topsy-Turvy* (also known as *The Purchase of the North Pole*). *Journey Through the Impossible* is the only piece where so many characters from other works—including both trilogies—appear together. The first half of Jules Verne's life and work culminates with *Journey Through the Impossible*, a mantle atop the two trilogies.

In 1882 all plays were checked by a governmental office before a work was produced; the manuscripts were manually copied by anonymous civil servants and archived. In 1978 Francis Lacassin searched the archives of the Censorship Office of the French Third Republic and discovered a copy of *Journey Through the Impossible*, ending nearly a century of speculation. The text was published in 1981 by the great

Vernian specialists François Raymond and Robert Pourvoyeur.[55] Until the archived copy came to light, Vernian scholars had only the reviews of the play to know what it was about and to imagine the text. To give an idea of what the play was like when staged in 1882, we have added two contemporary reviews. One, anonymous, was printed in the *New York Times* a few days after the play opened in Paris. The other is by French reviewer and playwright Arnold Mortier. Year after year, Mortier published a book where he reviewed the plays of the previous season. The two reviews we have included give a good idea of the set, the music, the ballets, and the public reception of the work.

Even in 1969, a former president of the Société Jules Verne published an article about the *Journey Through the Impossible*, based only on the reviews.[56] And in 1978, Robert Pourvoyeur, just before Lacassin's discovery, published a long article also based on the reviews,[57] where he pointed out the importance of the music in *Journey Through the Impossible*. Ballets characterize these *pièces à grand spectacle*, making them predecessors of modern music theater. Oscar de Lagoanère[58] wrote the music for *The Impossible*; the first ballet concludes Act I (the center of the Earth) and features a profusion of red costumes and fireworks. The second ballet takes place in Atlantis, where the indefinable sets mix many styles: Egyptian, Indian, Syrian, Roman, Greek, and Arab. The last ballet shows Altorians dancing and singing in brief costumes. According to the reviews, the third ballet was the best of the three.

The play can be read in two ways. The first and easiest—well-received by Parisian spectators—focuses on the music, the colors, the journey through diamond caves, the Nautilus, and the colossal cannon (for travel from Earth to Altor). The more difficult reading gets at the philosophy and the message of the work: glorifying the triumphant inventions of science, but showing that science, badly used, can bring death and devastation.

This publication is the first translation (in any language as far as we know) of *Journey Through the Impossible*, and is certainly the first to restore Act II, Scene 7 ("The Platform of the Nautilus"). Thus the complete script is now available to readers . . . and later perhaps to spectators.

Synopsis of the Play

Verne has selected the most striking incidents of his romantico-scientific productions, such as "Doctor Ox," *Journey to the Center of the Earth*, *From the Earth to the Moon*, and *Twenty Thousand Leagues under the Sea*.

In a little town in Denmark lives the Widow Traventhal, whose daughter Eva is betrothed to young George Hatteras. George is a son of that famous Captain Hatteras whose voyage in search of the North pole terminated fatally. His friends have always concealed the parentage: they feared lest the example of the father might tempt the child. But it is all in vain; no man can escape his destiny. The blood of the bold navigator courses through his veins; he thirsts after the unknown. Hatteras lives in the midst of maps and charts and globes, and in his delirium dreams of exploration such as none other has ever imagined. He would attempt the impossible.

"Quite mad!" say his fellow-citizens. "Certainly very sick!" reply Madame and Mademoiselle Traventhal, who immediately send for Dr. Ox and ask him to prescribe. Now, Dr. Ox is an excellent scientist by reputation but, instead of administering chloral or bromide of potassium, he works up the diseased brain of his patient, first, by revealing to Hatteras his connection with the deceased Arctic explorer; second, by the assurance that he can help Hatteras to realize his desire.

The doctor is a species of Mephistopheles; and he, too, is in love with Eva. The savant's scheme is truly diabolical. He administers an elixir that emancipates the youth from subjection to physical laws that hamper ordinary human beings, but his real object is to get rid of his rival by killing him or rendering him incurably mad. In vain does the organist Volsius try to snatch George from this sinister influence. He tries music, he tries argument, but he might as well have left both untried. George persists, and then, with a noble spirit of self-sacrifice, he assures the disconsolate maiden that he, too, will share the perils of her lover's peregrinations.

Volsius will protect Hatteras, he swears, in spite of himself, and this he does in a series of avatars wherein he appears as Professor Lidenbrock (Act I), Captain Nemo (Act II), Michel Ardan, and a citizen of the Planet Altor (Act III).

The struggle between the doctor and the musician is intended to illustrate the conflict between good and evil. But Eva is not altogether satisfied; she fears entrusting Hatteras to Volsius alone, and so she, too, with her a friend of the family, one Tartelet, the dancing master, takes a dose of the magic mixture, and in the twinkling of an eye Dr. Ox, Hatteras, Volsius, Eva, and the dancing master are transported to the foot of Mount Vesuvius, and there begins the first ballet.

The tourists, whose party is reinforced by a traveler from Denmark, whom they meet at Naples, Monsieur Valdemar by name, begin their excursions by a visit to the "entrails of the earth" in search of the "central fire." Three "entrails" are visited in this journey, of which a fissure in the volcano is the starting point. The first entrail is a rocky cavern, while the second appears to be made of granite. The third is represented by a most fantastic subterranean vegetation, with the atmosphere rendered peculiarly luminous, resulting from an under-ground rivulet of extraordinary light and color. These regions are inhabited by the Troglodytes, a degenerate class of beings, ugly, but picturesque, with long hair, mud-tinted faces, and silver hands.

Next step: The harbor of Goa, with Indian pavilions, and in the background the city and the sea. Here, Monsieur Valdemar, the funny man, does a monologue expressive of his satisfaction with the "diamond picked up 5,000 feet below the surface of the earth." Then the Nautilus, a cigar-shaped craft, steams in: the travelers go on board, and in the eleventh setting are seen seated around the hospitable table of Captain Nemo—the third incarnation of Volsius. The Nautilus plunges, and her passengers walk out of their cabins into the magic city of the Atlantides. The citizens of this realm are rising up in a revolution, and they want a king. Having chosen one of their own, they are about to crown him when the prophetess of Atlantis plots with Dr. Ox and Hatteras to make a coup d'état, which results in the selection of George and his immediate coronation, all serving as a pretext for more dancing, more marble staircases, porphyry columns, minarets, and stage props in general.

For the next part of the journey, the Gun Club, offers nothing specially interesting or original. The members amuse themselves by shooting pistols while the big gun is being made ready. A servant enters, and the Columbiad is prepared. "Gentlemen," he announces, "will the intending travelers kindly take seats in the shell!" With the exception of Dr. Ox, the party gets into the projectile and, the scene changing, the huge mortar. Just as the match is being applied, Monsieur Volsius rushes on the stage and insists on an excursion ticket, which is kindly granted by the Gun Club's committee. He gets in at the vent: an explosion is heard, and again the scene shifts to the planet Altor. The vehicle has reached its destination in safety; and the occupants are met by Maître Volsius as an Altorian in a long robe, to whom Valdemar and Tartelet make a political speech in explanation of the advantages and disadvantages of parliamentarianism, while their companions admire the architectural beauties of a planet where a cottage has a golden roof and walls encrusted with precious stones. Another discovery much impresses the party: the

Altorians are favored with two suns—one for the day, the other for the night.

It is in the marketplace of Altor that the third ballet of the play takes place. Suddenly, in the midst of mirth and joy, comes a terrible crash. A "meteoric comet" has struck the festive planet: everything crumbles away, the clouds gather, the thunder rolls, the lightning flashes, and Altor becomes a thing of the past. The excursionists escape the cataclysm. They return to Earth, where, in Andernak Castle, Hatteras, at first quite insane, recovers his reason, thanks to his betrothed, whose love triumphs over the jealous hate of the fatal doctor, after which comes the obligatory apotheosis in three transformations and the curtain falls.

Cast of Characters

MAIN CHARACTERS

Mme de Traventhal, a wealthy aristocrat living in Andernak Castle. Her money pays all expenses during the journey.

Eva, daughter of Mme de Traventhal and fiancée of George Hatteras

George, son of Captain Hatteras, the explorer who discovered the North Pole in *Journeys and Adventures of Captain Hatteras*, by Jules Verne. George wants to do more than his father: not an "Extraordinary Journey," but an "Impossible Journey."

Doctor Ox, scientist and chemist, evil character, from Verne's short story "Doctor Ox." He mentors George and pushes him to do the impossible.

Volsius, a good character who becomes Lidenbrock (from *Journey to the Center of the Earth*) in Act I, Nemo (from *Twenty Thousand Leagues under the Sea*) in Act II, and Michel Ardan (from *From the*

Earth to the Moon and *Around the Moon*) in Act III. Volsius protects
George and Eva, and fights against Dr. Ox.

Tartelet, friend of Mme de Traventhal and Eva, a comic character in
the play.

Valdemar, Danish citizen and the other comic character. He becomes
a friend of Tartelet.

SECONDARY CHARACTERS

In Andernak:

Niels, servant of Mme de Traventhal

In Naples:

Italian Innkeeper

In Goa:

Jeweller in Goa
First Hindu
Englishman (Captain Anderson)
A naval officer

In Atlantis:

A herald
Ammon (citizen of Atlantis)
Ascalis (citizen of Atlantis)
Electra (a prophetess)

At the Gun Club and at the Columbiad, in Florida:

First group of members of the Gun Club
Second group of members of the Gun Club
Barbicane, president of the Gun Club in Baltimore (from *From the
Earth to the Moon* and *Around the Moon*)

An Usher

J.T. Maston, secretary of the Gun Club in Baltimore (from *From the Earth to the Moon* and *Around the Moon*)

Members of the Gun Club

The employee of the telephone company

On the Planet Altor:

First Altorian

Second Altorian

Journey Through the Impossible

by

Jules Verne

TRANSLATED BY Edward Baxter

Act I
The Center of the Earth

—SCENE 1—
ANDERNAK CASTLE

The great hall of a Danish castle[1] in Saxon architectural style. Doors at the back and at the left. On the right, an organ[2] stands against the wall. It is night. Mme de Traventhal[3] is sitting at the left, working at a tapestry. Eva is sitting at a table, leafing through maps and books.

Eva: Here they are, the travel books and maps that poor George is always looking through. The pages are covered with notes that show only too clearly how disturbed his mind is. Look, grandma! There are pencil marks everywhere, scrawled in a shaky hand-writing. These travelers discovered the remotest regions of our globe and risked their lives to explore them from one pole to the other. But that would not have satisfied George's ambition. Look at these words written in the margin: "Onward! Farther! Still far-ther!" Ah! George will never find peace of mind again.

Mme de Traventhal: Eva, my dear girl, you mustn't give up hope. George loves you and he knows you love him. He's never known any family but ours since the misfortune that befell his father, who went insane in the course of his ambitious undertakings. But it's nearly twenty years now that George has been living with us in Andernak Castle. Under our care, he'll eventually control his overactive imagination. He'll understand that happiness is to be found here, in family life, and God will do the rest.

Eva: Let's hope so, grandma, let's hope so.

Mme de Traventhal: But it's important to me that he should never know who his parents were.

Eva: The son of Captain Hatteras,[4] the bold explorer who reached the North Pole, and came back only to end his days in a mental hospital. Oh, you're right! George must never know! His mind is already overwrought, and that knowledge might prove fatal to him.

Mme de Traventhal: Where is he now, the poor boy? What kind of a night did he have?

Eva: Still very restless. Our old friend Niels told me he paced up and down in his room for a long time, muttering incoherently. Everything in his mind is expressed in the words: "Onward! Farther still!" What can be done? Couldn't we consult a doctor?

Mme de Traventhal: I've thought of that. But just to make sure George won't know we're worried about him, the doctor will come to see me.

Eva: To see you?

Mme de Traventhal: Yes, I'm expecting him this morning. I asked that nice Mr. Tartelet[5] to call him.

Eva: Mr. Tartelet?

Mme de Traventhal: He seemed so happy to be able to do a favor for us.

Eva: Yes, he's a fine man. When he came here from Paris he had no letters of recommendation and no money. He said he was a dancing teacher.

Mme de Traventhal: A teacher of dancing and deportment, he said.

Eva: You made him welcome. In fact, you gave him a home, and since no one here has any interest in dancing. . . .

Mme de Traventhal: He stayed with us as a friend.

Eva: But a very worried friend, grandma, very tormented.

Mme de Traventhal: Why so?

Eva: It upsets his sensitive nature to be paid a salary when no one comes to his classes.

Mme de Traventhal: Good! But he's almost one of the family now, isn't he?

(Enter Tartelet *by a side door, carrying his violin under his arm.)*

Tartelet: Here I am, ladies.

Mme de Traventhal: Ah! Mr. Tartelet. Well?

Tartelet: The famous doctor will be here in a moment.

Mme de Traventhal: Many thanks, Mr. Tartelet.

Tartelet: Will there be anything else, ma'am?

Mme de Traventhal *(surprised)*: Anything else? What do you mean?

Tartelet: Is there any other little thing you might want me to do?

Eva: Want you to do, Mr. Tartelet?

Tartelet: Yes, miss, yes. You mustn't think that all I can do is dance entrechats and scrape the violin. An old bachelor like me, forced to fend for himself, has to know how to do many little odd jobs. I can repair damaged furniture, mend valuable porcelain, sew on buttons. If need be, I can even do a little laundry.

Eva *(laughing)*: You do laundry, Mr. Tartelet?

Tartelet: Yes, miss, but unfortunately, I know nothing about ironing.

Mm de Traventhal: Set your mind at rest, my dear Mr. Tartelet. We feel your affection for us . . . and . . . *(holding out her hand)* and that's enough for us.

Tartelet: That's enough for you. . . . It's enough for you, ma'am, but not enough for me. Every morning I arrive on time for my lesson, but—I never teach my lesson. And you still pay me.

Eva: Well, what if I don't feel like having a lesson?

Tartelet: In that case, miss, I ought not to feel like accepting a fee for it. For six months now I've been living in this castle. At the rate of one lesson a day, that makes one hundred and eighty lessons that I haven't taught. At two crowns a lesson, it adds up to a total of three hundred and sixty crowns that I've received, and which I now have the honor, ma'am, of returning to you. *(He takes his purse out of his pocket.)*

Eva: Please put that away, you naughty man.

Mme de Traventhal: Mr. Tartelet, I thought you considered yourself our friend.

Tartelet: I, your friend? That is a great honor, ma'am. I would be very glad, but—I wouldn't want to be paid two crowns a day for being your friend.

Mme de Traventhal: It's an advance on what we'll have to pay you later.

Tartelet: Later? I don't understand.

Mme de Traventhal: Well, for your future pupils.

Tartelet: My future pupils? I still don't understand.

Mme de Traventhal: But it's very simple. You know that George and Eva are engaged, and will be married some day—very soon perhaps—and later on *(lowering her voice)*—don't you see? A whole class of pretty little pupils.

Tartelet: Ah! Yes, yes, I see. I understand. Take young children in infancy, teach them to position their pretty little feet correctly as soon as they come into the world. Develop their charm in childhood to make sure they will also be charming as adolescents—what a joy that would be, what a dream, what happiness!

Mme de Traventhal: That dream will come true, Mr. Tartelet. So you see, you can't leave us. And besides, what would you do? Go back to Paris and try to find work?

Tartelet: To Paris? Oh no, ma'am, no! No one dances there any more. All they do is jump around.

Eva: They jump around?

Tartelet: Yes, miss, they do. And not only in the salons. They jump around in the banks, at the stock exchange, everywhere. We even have talented choreographers, famous dancers themselves, who get the prefects and ministers jumping around.

Mme de Traventhal: What's this you're telling us?

Eva: That means there's no more dancing in Paris.

Tartelet: In Paris, miss, in Paris, the only kind of dancing they know is the money dance.

Eva: Sh! Here comes George.

(Enter George stage left, looking sad and thoughtful. Without seeing anyone, he sits down at the table and leafs idly through the open books lying there.)

Eva *(aside)*: Oh! My poor darling!

Mme de Traventhal: You're right. He's more depressed than ever.

George *(placing his hands on the maps)*: Here's where they went, those incredible heroes, into the bowels of the earth, to the depths of the sea, through outer space! Lidenbrok,[6] Nemo,[7] Ardan,[8] where no one had ever set foot before. And that other one, Captain Hatteras, conqueror of the North Pole. Some mysterious attraction draws me even more closely to him. I feel strong enough to equal them, maybe even surpass them, but I've done nothing yet—nothing!

(He sits with his head in his hands, overcome.)

Eva *(going up to him)*: Your hand is burning, George.

George *(looking up)*: Eva! It's you! *(To* Mme de Traventhal*)* And you, grandmother.

Mme de Traventhal: Are you in pain, George?

George: Yes. I feel as if I'm being consumed by a constant fever, which no human medicine can cure.

Eva: Not even friendship?

Mme de Traventhal *(in a low voice, pointing to* Eva*)*: Not even love?

George: Eva! *(Going up to her)* Eva dear, you know I love you and that my heart is yours—and yours, too, grandmother. But my imagination is stronger than my heart. Every hour of the day and night it carries me away from this castle, far away from this country, beyond the ends of the earth and almost into unknown worlds. And I hear a voice calling me: "Forward, farther, still farther!"

Eva: Calm yourself, George, I beg you. Ah! If you really loved me. . . .

George: I do love you, Eva. Our two lives will be one some day—after my dreams have been realized. But until then I'm not completely yours. I feel it. First I must go where my destiny calls me.

Tartelet: And one would need exceptional legs to follow him.

Eva *(taking his hand)*: You're planning to leave us, then.

George: I'll come back to you, Eva.

Eva: And what if you don't find me here when you come back?

George: Not find you here! What do you mean?

Eva: I don't know. I just feel as if some danger is threatening me.

George: Danger? What danger?

Mme de Traventhal: What is it, girl? Speak up.

Eva: For some time now, whenever I leave the castle with old Niels, I've been followed by a man whose presence really terrifies me.

George: Who is this man?

Eva: I don't know, but he has strange, bizarre ways, and he frightens me. He seems to know in advance what I'm going to do and where I'm going to go.

George: And you say he follows you everywhere?

Eva: Everywhere, and the strange thing is that he only stops when I go into the church. There, at the threshold of the Holy Place, he gets an even stranger look on his face. His lips are twisted with bitter irony and an angry fire burns in his eyes.

George: And when you are in the church?

Eva: My soul becomes calm again, especially when Master Volsius plays the organ.

George: Master Volsius?

Eva: Yes, the new organist. I believe he's attached to the cathedral at Aalborg.[9] He's a musical genius. I'd almost say he's a superhuman artist. When he plays the accompaniment for the psalms of penitence, you can see the darkness of hell open up before your eyes. When he sings of the glory of the Almighty, you are carried off to Paradise itself. The walls recede, as if by some marvellous spell, the church vanishes, and his genius calls forth a heavenly vision, surrounded by the most sublime harmonies.

Mme de Traventhal: Yes, Eva, yes. I've felt the same ecstasy as you have while listening to him.

Eva: It's more than ecstasy. You can see what that great artist is trying to express. You can see it, grandma, you can really see it.

Tartelet: And I've seen it too. Yes, yes, I've seen this miracle, and I've been assured that this man is more than a peerless organist. He produces the most miraculous sounds with my poor old violin. He could make houses dance.

(Enter Niels.*)*

Niels: Madam, the doctor is here.

George *(hastily)*: A doctor?

Mme de Traventhal: Yes, my dears, I've sent for a doctor to come and see me. I heard that there is a very famous doctor in Aalborg right now, and I've asked him to come. He will give me some good advice—and you, too, Eva, and George and Tartelet.

Tartelet: But I'm not sick.

Mme de Traventhal: People are always sick—more or less. I've observed that doctors have the greatest success. . . .

Tartelet: With healthy people.

Mme de Traventhal: Show in Dr. Ox.[10]

George: Is this the Dr. Ox who carried out those extraordinary experiments that doubled people's vital capacity under the influence of oxygen?

Mme de Traventhal: Exactly.

George: I'm curious to see him.

Tartelet *(aside)*: Mr. George doesn't need any extra oxygen, though. He needs to have a little less of it.

Niels *(announcing)*: Dr. Ox.

Tartelet: Some charlatan, no doubt.

(Enter Dr. Ox, *through the door at the back.)*

Eva *(aside, terrified)*: What's this I see? It's him, the man who keeps following me!

Ox (*to* Mme de Traventhal): You sent for me, madam. Here I am.

Mme de Traventhal: Doctor, I heard that you were in Aalborg, where your great reputation has preceded you, and I wish to have your opinion. . . .

Ox: About this young lady, perhaps.

Eva (*hastily*): No, no, not about me.

Mme de Traventhal: Eva is in excellent health.

Ox: Are you quite sure? See how pale and nervous she is. (*He takes her hand.*)

Eva: Oh!

Ox: This delicate hand trembles in mine. (Eva *quickly pulls her hand away, but he seizes it again.*) It's like fear, or terror, even. But we'll calm that.

Eva (*moving away from him*): You're mistaken. I'm not frightened or terrified. (*Aside*) My intuition tells me this man has brought misfortune to our house.

George (*to the doctor*): Doctor, I'm happy to meet you. I've followed your wonderful experiments—from a distance, but with great interest.

Ox: Indeed?

George: Increasing the oxygen content of the air, transforming the body and the soul! Doubling, even tripling, the vital capacity! That is magnificent.

Ox: It's also very simple, sir. The human body is like a burning stove. I simply found a way of putting on a little more coal. But let's get straight to the point, sir. You're the one I'm here to treat.

George: Me?

Mme de Traventhal: Doctor, what are you talking about?

Ox: There's no point in beating about the bush, madam. This young man's health is a matter of great concern to you.

Mme de Traventhal: Yes, of course.

Ox: And to you also, miss.

Eva *(coldly)*: George is my fiancé, sir.

Ox *(aside)*: Your fiancé. *(Aloud)* Now, his mind harbors dreams that seem insane to you, and you want to cure him of the grandiose ideas that are simmering in his brain.

George: So that's it. They brought you here to see me.

Ox: You, and no one else.

Mme de Traventhal: Who told you that, sir?

Ox: In this country, madam, everyone knows your name, and this young man's story is known to everyone but himself.

George: What is he talking about?

Ox: You expect me to make him well. All right, I'll undertake to cure him. But don't expect me to turn his thoughts away from the glorious goal he's been pursuing for so long.

Eva: What do you mean?

Ox: Do you think that by compressing a gas you can prevent it from exploding? Of course not. On the contrary, let him give free rein to his ambition. Don't stifle his noble rapture. Let him say how far he wants to go, and then let us try to prepare the way for him.

George: What I want, doctor, is to surpass what has been done by the heroes whose names are written in these books, to go beyond the frontiers that they could not cross. Professor Lidenbrok penetrated into the bowels of the earth. I want to go all the way to its central fire. Captain Nemo, in his *Nautilus*,[11] sought independence in the depths of the sea. I want to live in that element, and travel through it from pole to pole. The daring Michel Ardan enclosed himself in a capsule and went into orbit several thousand leagues above the earth. I want to fly from one planet to another. That's what I want, doctor. Is it impossible?

Ox *(in a powerful voice)*: No!

Eva: How dare you say that, sir!

Ox: No! A thousand times no! You will know what you aspire to know, and your eyes will see what you aspire to see, if your courage does not fail.

George: It will never fail. Go on—but isn't this all an empty dream?

Ox: I will lead you into reality itself.

George: Into reality!

Ox *(taking a vial from his pocket)*: See this vial. Anyone who drinks a few drops of this potion will be carried away with the speed of a thunderbolt, and under conditions of a new life, to regions where man is forbidden to go. There will be no more intervals of time and distance. Men will fly as fast as lightning. Days will go by in a few seconds, years in a few minutes.

George: And will I reach the earth's central fire?

Ox: Yes!

George: And the bottom of the ocean?

Ox: Yes!

George: And go as far into outer space as I want?

Ox: Yes!

George: Ah! That would truly be an impossibility.

Ox: An impossibility that you will accomplish, because I will make your body capable of going unharmed to places where men burn, to places where they drown. You'll be able to breathe even where there is no more air to breathe. You'll be carried away as if by a whirlwind, and return as the hero of the impossible, the hero who explored the most unfathomable mysteries of nature.

Eva: To try to do something like that is not only insane, George, it's criminal, it's sacrilegious.

Mme de Traventhal (*terrified*): Yes, my daughter is right. In heaven's name, sir, say no more.

George: Let him speak, grandmother, let him speak. Doctor, I believe in you. I'm ready to follow you.

Eva: George, you'd be deserting us, deserting the woman who took you in and loved you as her own child. And deserting me, too, George!

Ox (*shouts*): Go ahead, beg, weep, soften his heart, weaken his soul, cast him back into his childhood, this son of Hatteras, just when I was about to make a man of him.

Mme de Traventhal (*to* Eva): Good God!

George (*shouts*): Son of Hatteras, did you say? I'm the son of Hatteras, the son of the daring navigator who made his way to the North Pole?

Ox: Yes, yes, that illustrious man was your father.

George: My father! The man whose wonderful tales I read so avidly. The man I always wanted to imitate.

Ox: And you will surpass him if you want to.

George: Ah! Nothing will ever stop me now.

Mme de Traventhal: Alas! All is lost.

Eva: This man is the evil genius of our family.

Ox (*aside*): Now he is mine!

(*Enter* Master Volsius.)

Master Volsius: Excuse me, ladies and gentlemen, am I at the home of Mme de Traventhal?

Mme de Traventhal: You are, sir. May I know . . . ?

Volsius: Madam, as I was leaving the cathedral I happened to find this prayer book. Thinking it belonged to someone in the castle, I took the liberty. . . . Perhaps it is yours, madam?

Mme de Traventhal: No.

Volsius *(to* Ox*)*: Is it yours, then, sir? Yes, it must be yours.

Ox *(drawing back)*: Mine?

Volsius: Take it, sir, do take it.

Ox *(still drawing back)*: Mine? This book? No, I tell you, no!

Volsius: Oh! Don't be afraid. It won't burn your fingers.

Eva *(approaching)*: It's my prayer book. I left it behind in church this morning. Thank you for bringing it back to me.

Ox: But who are you, sir?

Volsius: I, sir? I am the organist at the cathedral.

Eva: Master Volsius!

All: Master Volsius!

George: Volsius, the great musician!

Volsius: Volsius, the humble organist, sir.

Ox *(aside)*: What's he doing here?

Eva: Ah, sir, we have heard you many times in the cathedral, and been thrilled by your sublime harmonies!

Volsius: I am only a poor musician, miss.

Mme de Traventhal: The doors of Andernak Castle will always be open to you.

Ox *(aside)*: We'll see about that.

Mme de Traventhal *(introducing)*: My granddaughter Eva.

Volsius: How do you do?

Mme de Traventhal *(introducing* George*)*: Her fiancé, George. . . .

George *(hastily)*: George Hatteras.

Volsius: The son of the famous Captain Hatteras?

George *(excitedly)*: Yes, yes, he's my father, and I'm going to equal his achievements, and even surpass his discoveries, thanks to the learned Dr. Ox.

Volsius *(turning to Ox)*: Dr. Ox! I have heard a great deal about Dr. Ox. I hope I find you well, Dr. Ox?

Ox *(turning his back on him)*: Very well . . . Master . . . Volsius.

Volsius: They say, doctor, that you have the power to make the human body capable of going through the impossible.

Ox: And what they say is true, Master Volsius.

Volsius: Even capable of understanding those mysteries that God seems to have reserved for Himself alone.

Ox: Yes, we shall penetrate those impenetrable mysteries.

Volsius: And you are offering the son of Captain Hatteras an opportunity to carry on in his own name the attempts that failed, even in mythology—an opportunity to repeat the experiments of Icarus?

Ox: Yes, but without destroying his wings.

Volsius: The adventures of Prometheus?

Ox: Yes, but with no danger from the vulture's talons.

Volsius: And the efforts of the Titans?[12]

Ox: Yes, but with no danger of being struck by Jupiter's thunderbolt.

Volsius: In fact, then, you are very strong.

Tartelet *(aside)*: My goodness, it seems to me that the organist is the cleverest of them all.

Ox: I think, Master Volsius, that you are making fun of the power this potion bestows. Well, drink a few drops of it, and you will have no more doubts.

Volsius: Thank you, doctor, but I have no need of it.

George *(reaching for the vial)*: Give it to me, then. Give it to me.

Volsius *(stopping his arm)*: Young man, the vain attempts I have just mentioned may not have touched your soul. No one believes in this fictitious mythology. But open the holy scriptures and there you will find more ambitious arrogance, more audacious rebellions—and more dreadful punishments. And they are real, and so terrible that Dr. Ox himself would be afraid to face them.

Ox *(angrily)*: What punishments? Tell me. Answer me!

Volsius *(gently)*: Excuse me, doctor. A thousand pardons. I am not expressing myself. . . . I can only speak clearly, they say, with my fingers. I'll try to make myself understood. *(He goes to the organ and sits down.)* I'll try to show you to what abysmal depths sacrilegious pride can sink.

Ox: What is he going to do?

Eva: O Lord, inspire him. Save George. O Lord, Lord, save us all.

(The organ sounds.)

⌐SCENE 2⌐

THE FALLEN ANGEL

The back of the hall is open and the sides have disappeared, to reveal the decor representing an angel falling. Dr. Ox backs away at first, then returns upstage and watches.

Ox: It's the angel falling.

Volsius *(going up to him)*: This is the punishment for pride.

Ox: You're a wonderful musician, Master Volsius, but the fallen angel fell gloriously. The grandeur of his fall lent almost as much brilliance to his name as did his daring rebellion. He won glory. Glory above all!

George: Yes, yes. Glory, glory!

Ox: That's where I will lead you.

Volsius: Yes, to glory, or to madness.

Mme de Traventhal: Madness!

Volsius: But wherever he goes, he will find me in his way.

(*Exit* Volsius *and* Eva.)

Ox: Come, George Hatteras, take this vial and drink!

(George *drinks.*)

Eva (*snatching the vial from him*): Well, I won't desert you, George. I'll share the dangers.

(*She drinks, too, and throws away the vial.*)

George: Eva, what have you done?

Ox: Both of them! All right, so be it!

Tartelet (*picks up the vial*): What? Just with this potion, you could. . . . (*He drinks.*) Let's go, then.

— S C E N E   3 —

T H E   I N N

The terrace of an Italian inn, with vine-covered pillars. On the right, an inn with doors and windows. Pergola and benches on the terrace. In the left background can be seen Vesuvius,[13] its crater wreathed in smoke. To the right extends the beginning of the Bay of Naples.[14] It is daytime.

(*Enter* George, Eva, Ox, *and* Tartelet.)

Tartelet: Where are we? I don't see the town of Aalborg, or the spires of the cathedral.

George (*to* Ox): Where are we, doctor?

Ox: In Naples, not far from Vesuvius. You can see its summit.

George: Vesuvius! That's the crater where Professor Lidenbrok came out.

Ox: And the crater through which we will penetrate to the center of our globe.

Eva: Right to the fiery lake! George! It's time for you to stop.

George: Don't be afraid, Eva.

Tartelet: Dear me, I seem to be hungry. You can't travel six hundred leagues without a little something to eat.

Ox: Here's an inn. Call out, and someone will serve you. Meanwhile, we'll get ready for our dangerous descent.

Tartelet: Get ready! But why? After all, you can cover hundreds of leagues in one leap.

Ox (*to* George): Are we simply going to reach our goal without seeing or understanding or studying anything?

George: No, of course not.

Ox: Do you want to remain in ignorance of all the secrets and mysteries in order to avoid all the dangers?

George: No, no!

Ox: Come on, then.

Tartelet: Go ahead, you'll meet me back here. *(Exit George, Eva, and Ox.)* Now, let's call out. Hello! Waiter!

(Enter the innkeeper.)

Innkeeper *(watching the three disappear)*: Well, well. A traveler.

Tartelet: Yes indeed. Come over here, waiter. You look surprised.

Innkeeper: Yes sir, very surprised.

Tartelet: Are you all alone here, then, waiter?

Innkeeper: Yes, except for a Dane who arrived yesterday.

Tartelet: A Dane. I once knew a Dane, a Great Dane he was, very tall and handsome, with splendid ears and a long snout. A beautiful dog.

Innkeeper: No, no. This one is a young man.

Tartelet: Oh, I see. A two-legged Dane. Tell me, waiter, what can you bring me to eat?

Innkeeper: There's nothing left at the moment. The Dane ate it all.

Tartelet: That's all right. Give me some anyway—and not too well done.

Innkeeper: Right away, sir. *(Exit.)*

(Enter Valdemar, followed by the innkeeper.)

Valdemar *(nodding to Tartelet)*: Ah, that was a good lunch I had! Maybe even a little too good.

Tartelet: It's the Dane. And he doesn't have a long snout.

Valdemar: Well, well. A foreigner. Mr. . . . uh?

Tartelet *(nodding to him)*: Sir! . . . *(Aside)* What an awkward way of speaking! He doesn't even know how to greet people properly.

Valdemar: Good day, sir. Mr. . . . uh? Usually, when people meet someone in their travels, even at the ends of the earth or farther, they soon get acquainted. May I be so bold as to ask your name?

Tartelet: Professor Tartelet.

Valdemar *(aside)*: A professor! He's a scientist! *(Aloud)* What country are you from, sir?

Tartelet: I'm French. I was born in Asnières.[15]

Valdemar: Asnières. Ah, yes, Asnières de Bigorre.[16] I know that place.

Tartelet: No you don't.

Valdemar: Are you married, Mr. Tartelet?

Tartelet: No, why do you ask?

Valdemar: Then you don't have any little Tartelets?

Tartelet: No.

Valdemar *(laughs)*: No little Tarts?

Tartelet: No little. . . . *(Aside)* Who is this big oaf? *(He looks at Valdemar's feet.)* Ah, those feet!

Valdemar: I beg your pardon?

Tartelet: Out, young man, out.

Valdemar *(surprised)***:** Out? He's sending me away. He wants to be alone.

Tartelet: Where are you going?

Valdemar: You told me to go out.

Tartelet: I meant you should point your toes out. It's what we call the choreographic angle.

Valdemar: The what?

Tartelet *(touching him with the tip of his bow)***:** Farther apart. Farther, farther. *(Valdemar nearly falls down.)* That's fine, just like that.

Valdemar: Oh, you think that's fine, do you? A funny kind of scientist you are!

Tartelet: I have the honor of speaking to Mr. . . . ?

Valdemar: Axel[17] Valdemar, from Copenhagen.

Tartelet: Excellent! Well, Mr. Axel Vladimir. . . .

Valdemar: Excuse me, it's Valdemar.

Tartelet: All right, all right.

Valdemar: And you've come from . . . ?

Tartelet: From Aalborg.

Valdemar: You came by train?

Tartelet: No.

Valdemar: By ship?

Tartelet: No.

Valdemar: By stage coach?

Tartelet: No, I ran.

Valdemar: You ran?

Tartelet: On electricity.

Valdemar: You ran on electricity!

Tartelet: Yes.

Valdemar: And where are you going?

Tartelet (*pointing to the ground*): Down there!

Valdemar: Into the cellar?

Tartelet: Lower.

Valdemar: Lower my voice? Why? Is anyone listening to us?

Tartelet: Underground. To the center.

Valdemar: To the center of the earth?

Tartelet: Through the crater.

Valdemar: That's not possible.

Tartelet: It's not possible, but we'll do it, my friend. Your feet! (*Correcting his position*) Your feet!

Valdemar: (*Aside*) Again! A funny kind of scientist he is!

Tartelet: And you, Mr. Vladimir?

Valdemar: Val . . . demar, if you please.

Tartelet: Very well. Now it's your turn to tell me about yourself. Where are you going, Mr. Vladimir?

Valdemar (*aside*): He insists on calling me Vladimir! (*Aloud*) I'm going to a place, Mr. Tartelet, where a man can make his fortune.

Tartelet: That's a place I haven't found yet.

Valdemar: You see, I'm in love with a charming young lady in Copenhagen, Miss Babichok.[18]

Tartelet: And naturally, Miss Babichok is not in love with you, Mr. Vladimir.

Valdemar: Vladimir again! I told you my name is Valdemar.

Tartelet: Ah! Excuse me, young man. It's just that there are some names I can't manage to pronounce, and I don't think I'd ever be able to say yours. I'd rather call you Matthew. Is that all right?

Valdemar: Matthew suits me fine. I once had a good friend named Matthew.

Tartelet: So did I.

Valdemar: He was an astronomer.

Tartelet: Matthew Laensberg, it was. You said your name is Valdemar?

Valdemar: Oh, so you can say it now. Good!

Tartelet: Excuse me, I was mistaken. You were saying that Babichok . . . ?

Valdemar: Is madly in love with me. Ah! What a woman! What a soul! What a heart! And beautiful! When I think about it, I get palpitations[19]—right here. *(With great feeling)* Do you know about palpitations? I think you call them "battements" in French.

Tartelet: Do I know about battements? Of course. In ballet there are big ones and small ones.

Valdemar *(surprised)*: Big ones and small ones?

Tartelet: You raise one leg and move it up and down, while the other leg supports the whole weight of the body. Try it.

Valdemar: Try what?

Tartelet: Some battements. Like this. *(He demonstrates.)* Try it.

Valdemar: *(Aside)* He's not well! That isn't the kind of palpitation I'm talking about. What a funny kind of scientist!

Tartelet: I'm wondering why you haven't married Babichok, if she loves you so much.

Valdemar: There were two obstacles to our union. In the first place, Babichok considered me too fat and too thin.

Tartelet: How can that be?

Valdemar: Too fat physically and too thin financially.

Tartelet: I see.

Valdemar: Well, yes, I am a little on the plump side, I told her, but when it comes to something you love, the more of it you have, the better. Perhaps she might have gone along with my corpulence, seeing that she was rather skinny herself. Between us, we would have averaged out to make a nice little well-padded couple.

Tartelet: Yes, one would have made up for the other. The only problem left, then, was. . . .

Valdemar: Money! She simply would not let go of that idea. She loves me too much. Valdemar, she would say, I want you to be rich, very rich. I want you to have a fine carriage and beautiful hair—I mean beautiful horses—and beautiful hair, too, of course, and a lovely hotel where I can adore my idol to my heart's content. But to see you in poverty, in misery, I couldn't stand it. I'd rather put up with someone else than endure the pain of sharing your poverty. Tell me, Mr. Tartelet, is that not true love?

Tartelet: That is perfect love. First class.

Valdemar: And so I left in the hope of making my fortune, and by traveling to develop the brilliant qualities of my soul.

Tartelet: You did the right thing. Matthew! Your feet!

Valdemar: I've seen many countries in my time, and benefited from that experience, if I may be so bold as to say so. I've studied the way of life, I've observed the costu . . . the customs, and I've jotted down all my poetic impressions in this notebook.

Tartelet: That must be a remarkable notebook.

Valdemar: Look at this, now. "France: admirable country. Paris: admirable country."

Tartelet: That's brief and to the point.

Valdemar: I have to make myself understood. "In Paris, we ate beef, veal, and mutton. Switz . . ."[20]

Tartelet: Swiss mutton?

Valdemar: No, no. There's a period in there. "Switzerland: admirable country. Geneva: admirable country, ate veal, mutton, and beef. Italy: Rome. Rome!"

Tartelet: Ate veal, beef, and mutton.

Valdemar: No. I let you say that, just to be polite, but there isn't any there. All they eat there is goat's meat, the way they eat macaroni here.

Tartelet: And you're writing all these impressions for Miss Babichok?

Valdemar: Naturally. It will be interesting for her, and for Cousin Finderup,[21] who stayed behind with her.

Tartelet: Aha! There's Cousin Finderup, is there?

Valdemar: Yes. He's a friend of mine. A good lad. He's supposed to write to me at each of my stops, with news of my fiancée. As soon as I've made my fortune. . . .

Tartelet: Well, have you made it yet?

Valdemar: Not yet, but I'm not discouraged. I'll do it. For her, mind you, I'll undertake the impossible.

Tartelet: The impossible. That's exactly where we're going. Will you come with us?

Valdemar: Where?

Tartelet: There. Down below.

Valdemar: In the cellar?

Tartelet: To the center of the earth.

Valdemar: What for?

Tartelet: Why, to make our fortune. Isn't that the general storehouse of valuable things? Silver, gold, diamonds? Don't the most precious things in the world come from the bowels of the earth?

Valdemar: That's true, yes. It's the central treasure house. All you have to do is help yourself. But I don't have the key.

Tartelet: We have it!

Valdemar: And will you take me with you?

Tartelet: Yes, if you agree to drink a few drops of a certain potion. It will take you there in a second.

Valdemar: Will we be running?

Tartelet: Running on electricity.

Valdemar: And where is this potion?

Tartelet: I have a vial of it here. I drank some by mistake, but you'll drink it out of ambition.

Valdemar: Ah, Mr. Tartelet, I'm so fortunate to have met you! One drop. Just one little drop.

Tartelet: All right, but on one condition.

Valdemar: I agree to it in advance.

Tartelet: For two hours a day, you must place your feet in the third position.

Valdemar: What do you call the third position?

Tartelet: Look. Like this.

Valdemar *(He is surprised, but obeys)*: All right, I'll do it. But what good does it do you if I place my feet in the third position? You're a professor.

Tartelet: A dancing teacher, my friend.

Valdemar: A dancing teacher! And I thought you were a scientist!

Tartelet: Let's go and have a drop of that potion.

Valdemar: Yes, yes, a drop. Let's go and have a drop. *(Exit.)*

(Enter George, Ox, and Eva.)

George: Everything is ready. If there are risks to be run, you won't tremble?

Eva: No, of course not.

Ox *(to George):* Do you want to go?

George: Right now. There's the crater of Vesuvius, open to anyone brave enough to go down into it. Even if it were to close behind us, what would it matter? Let's go.

Ox: All right, then. To the center of the earth!

(Enter Master Volsius, disguised as Professor Lidenbrok.)

Volsius: To the center of the earth! Ah! Those are great and resounding words. And the hope of getting there, it seems to me, is a wonderful madness. Ah!

George: To whom have we the honor of speaking, sir?

Volsius: Professor Lidenbrok.

George: Professor Lidenbrok! You're the one who went. . . .

Volsius: Several hundred leagues under the earth, and no more, because it would have been impossible to go farther. And you find me here in Naples, within sight of Vesuvius, because a lava eruption carried me back up to the surface of the earth. It looked like a beautiful country to me, and I've decided to stay here for a while.

Ox: So, then, professor, you declare that it's impossible to go beyond the limits where you yourself were forced to stop.

Volsius *(laughing):* Exactly, sir. Exactly.

George: Is it forbidden, then, to try to win glory by a route that others have not been able to follow?

Volsius: Ah! That route is already marked out, sir. Parallel to the crater of Vesuvius, whose smoke you can see from here, there is another crater, an extinct one, which will take you where I went, if you feel so inclined.

Ox: We have to go in farther than that.

Volsius (*laughing*): Farther! Ah!

George: And we will.

Volsius: I stopped, gentlemen, when it was impossible to go any farther.

Ox (*sarcastically*): When you didn't dare go any farther.

Volsius: You think so! Upon my word, gentlemen, you are very brave. Your bold attempt fills me with enthusiasm and makes me want to start the journey over again with you.

George: Please do.

Eva: Oh yes, come, sir, do come. I don't know why, but I find your presence reassuring.

Volsius (*hesitating*): Well, it's decided, then. You want to go. . . .

Ox: To the center of the globe.

Volsius: I don't know why you risk your lives in such ventures, but I'll go with you and be your guide.

Ox: Come, then.

Eva: George, in heaven's name!

Volsius (*aside to* Eva): Let him go, miss. There are limits at which they will be forced to acknowledge human frailty, and they will not go beyond them. Come, my child, come.

(*Exit all.*)

— SCENE 4 —

FIVE HUNDRED LEAGUES UNDERGROUND

The stage represents an immense crypt, with depressions and openings on all sides, as far as the eye can see. Stalactites hang everywhere. Negotiable rocks, at the rear, make it possible to get down to the floor of these natural catacombs. George, Ox, Volsius, *and* Eva *are standing on the rocks.*

(*Enter* Tartelet *and* Valdemar.)

Tartelet: Hurry along, young Valdemar.

Valdemar (*appearing at the top of the rocks*)**:** Here I am! Here I am!

Tartelet: Damn! This road isn't good for a dancer's legs. (*To* Valdemar)*:* Be very careful not to twist an ankle.

Valdemar: Don't worry.

Ox: Come on, George Hatteras, onward, ever onward!

George: I'm right behind you, doctor. This is the abyss. It draws me on, and I'll go down to the very bottom of it.

(*They begin to descend.*)

Volsius (*to* Eva)**:** Don't be afraid, my child. This is not where the danger lies.

Eva: I'm not afraid for myself, but only for him.

Volsius: We are going to stop here for a bit.

George: Where are we?

Volsius: Why, at my home.

Ox: Indeed! This, I believe, is the farthest point reached by Master Lidenbrok.

Volsius: I might mention, if anyone is interested, that these caverns lie under central Europe, under France, and more precisely, at the point where we are standing now, under Paris.

Valdemar: Under Paris! Directly over my head is Paris, which I have visited with great affection, and the noise of that great city cannot be heard. *(A few distant rumblings are heard.)* Yes, it can! It sounds like a great rattling of carriages. We must be right under "accident corner."[22]

Eva *(to* Volsius*)*: But what is this noise?

Volsius: It's a rumbling that occurs at intervals deep inside the earth.

Valdemar: It's an earthquake! Let's get away from here. *(Exit.)*

Ox: Well, George Hatteras, what do you think of these immense spaces going on and on forever under oceans and continents, and containing cities and mountains? Did you expect to find a whole underground vegetation here, where the warm and humid environment turns the humblest of earth's plants into trees? Or this air, made luminous by pressure, which lights up the silent catacombs?

Volsius: Surely the contemplation of these wonders is enough to satisfy your ambitions for travel.

George: What would be the use of the new vital power that Dr. Ox has given our bodies if we were only going where others have gone before, where you yourself have gone? This is simply the extraordinary,[23] not the impossible.

Ox *(aside)*: Good, good!

(Valdemar utters a loud shout offstage.)

Eva: What can that be?

Tartelet: It's Valdemar's voice.

(Enter Valdemar.)

Valdemar *(terrified)*: Ah! Here you are!

Tartelet: What happened?

Valdemar (*showing him a stone*): This stone. . . . Do you see this stone?

Tartelet: That's a funny-looking stone.

Valdemar: It's not an ordinary stone, so I'm keeping it. But another thing that's unusual is the force with which it was thrown at my back.

Tartelet: Thrown? By whom?

Valdemar: By whom? That's what I'd like to know. There must be people here. And feel how heavy it is for its size.

Volsius: Everything is heavy here, young man.

Valdemar: What do you mean, everything is heavy here?

Ox: Of course. It's the natural effect of gravity.

Valdemar: Gravity?

Volsius: And if we reached the center, even your wallet would become so heavy it would make a hole in your pocket.

Valdemar: My wallet? Mine? As heavy as that? Now that would be a surprise.

Ox: And that's not all. Even the acoustics are different in this place where the air is under enormous pressure.

George: You mean that noises and sounds take on a tremendous intensity here?

Tartelet: So they do! When young Valdemar shouted just now, it sounded like cattle bellowing.

Valdemar: Cattle bellowing!

Tartelet: Well then, the violin I use for my dancing lessons would have a completely different tone here.

Volsius: Try it.

Tartelet: Right away. *(He picks up his violin and plays a gavotte with a surprisingly powerful sound.)*

Valdemar: That's amazing!

Tartelet: It's wonderful. Let's keep on playing.

(While Tartelet *is playing, a few creatures with bizarre faces, very low foreheads, a wild look in their eyes, and disheveled hair, appear between the rocks upstage, listening and showing signs of the greatest surprise.)*

Eva *(sees them and screams)*: Oh! Look at those monsters!

George *(moving upstage)*: Good God!

Eva: George! George! Stop!

*(*Tartelet *stops playing. The monsters disappear.)*

Ox: Yes, stay here. Anyway, as you see, they've disappeared.

George: What are these strange creatures?

Ox: This is the first of the mysteries that will be revealed to us. In the subterranean depths there's a whole population of living creatures.

George: A whole population!

Valdemar: A whole population!

Tartelet: Of living creatures! All right, then, we'll introduce them to the elementary principles of the dance.

Valdemar: Perhaps it was one of those gentlemen who threw the stone at me.

George: But how could a race of human beings have come into being and live way down here?

Volsius: Ask the learned Dr. Ox to answer that question.

Ox: Nothing could be more simple. All that was needed was for some inhabitants of the earth to be swallowed up here during one of the natural catastrophes that occurred thousands of years ago. They probably populated these vast solitary spaces, and their descendants, gradually modified by the environment in which they lived, lost their resemblance to the human race and became the lower creatures that you have just seen.[24]

Valdemar: Really!

Eva: It seemed to me just now that music had a sort of fascination for them.

Volsius: Yes, that's true.

George: What became of them? Let's go and look for them.

Eva: No, no!

Ox: What we need to find now is the route that will take us to our goal.

(A loud subterranean noise is heard.)

George: Listen to those noises coming through the earth's crust.

Valdemar: It's having convulsions now.

Ox: Soon, perhaps, the fire will open a path for us, leading from the earth to the crater of Vesuvius.

Volsius: And would you dare to travel that path?

George: Yes, yes.

Ox: We will dare!

Volsius: As I told you before, this goes beyond recklessness, it's . . . .

Ox: It's courage, plain and simple. Do you know what courage is, Professor Lidenbrok?

Volsius: Go wherever your pride drives you, then. *(To Eva)* I will pray fervently for you, you poor child. You are the soul of resignation, virtue, and piety. *(To Ox)* Do you know what piety and virtue are, Dr. Ox? *(Exit.)*

Eva: He's going away.

Ox: Let him go. He can spare us his cowardly advice. *(Another noise, louder than before.)* Listen, listen again. The route we're looking for will open up in that direction.

George: Come. We'll look for it together.

Eva: George. *(Exit Ox and George.)* George!

Valdemar: I think the other one was wiser. I'll try to catch up with him. *(Exit on the other side.)*

Eva: Ah! He doesn't even hear my voice.

Tartelet: That was a bad idea of your grandmother's, to call this damned doctor to the castle.

Eva: He would have come anyway, my friend, sooner or later.

Tartelet: What do you mean?

Eva: Sooner or later, he would have taken over George's imagination in the way he did, not to give him peace of mind, not to cure him, but to destroy him.

Tartelet: And to what end?

Eva: This man is the one who was always following me.

Tartelet: Him! Ah! Now I understand. He has the audacity to love you. Ah! Dr. Ox, what a pretty dance this dancing master would teach you, if only I could!

Eva: Don't attack him, my friend. He has some strange, supernatural power. *(Enter Ox upstage.)* Everything about him terrifies me: his imperious, dominating voice, the irresistible fascination of his glance. (Ox, *who has slowly come downstage, now approaches* Tartelet.)

Tartelet: It's true that the expression in his eyes is strangely diabol. . . .

Eva: Him!

Tartelet *(catches sight of Ox staring him in the face)*: Strangely diabol. . . . No. . . . I . . . I mean.

(Ox holds out his arm and gestures to him to leave.)

Tartelet: Allow me, doctor. . . . You wish. . . . You want. . . . *(Aside)* Oh! That look! That look!

Ox: Leave us!

Eva: Don't go, Mr. Tartelet.

Ox *(more imperiously than before, and looking* Tartelet *straight in the face)*: Do as I say!

Eva: No, no!

Ox *(as before)*: Leave us! I want you to leave.

Tartelet: What is the matter with me? I try, but I can't. . . . I can't. . . .

(He backs out.)

Eva *(calling)*: George, George!

Ox: George is far away. He can't hear you.

Eva: I'll find a way to get to him. *(Calling.)* George!

Ox *(blocking her way)*: I have to talk to you, Eva. Do you know why I used to follow you around wherever you went? Why I was always wandering around your home?

Eva: I don't want to know!

Ox: Because I love you.

Eva *(sarcastically)*: You love me? You?

Ox: I didn't come to Andernak Castle for your grandmother or your fiancé George. I came for you, and no one else. I wanted to be close to you. I wanted to see you and hear you, because I love you.

Eva: That's enough! Not another word!

Ox: And do you know why I told George who his father was, why I pushed him along this path, why I gave him the power to accomplish all these dreams? Because I don't want George to become your husband. *(His voice rises.)* And because I love you.

Eva: When George finds out what your intentions are, and why you're pushing him along toward this impossible world, he'll come to his senses and drive you away like an evil genie that has finally been unmasked.

Ox: You won't tell him, Eva. That would set us against each other, like two rivals. And you know very well that the struggle would be more dreadful for him than for me.

Eva: I will speak. . . .

Ox: Then you'll kill him. I'll have no further reason to drive him mad. You will have driven him to his death.

Eva *(terrified)***:** My God! George! George! This man would kill you.

Ox: Understand what I'm saying, Eva. I love you. I love you!

Eva: Ah! Don't profane that word. Go ahead, threaten me! I prefer your anger to your threats.

Ox: Very well, so be it. Your pleading is a waste of time. But remember my final words. Soon you'll come yourself and implore me to have pity on George. You'll beg me to stop him on the road he's following. You'll ask me to spare his sanity . . . his life. But it will be too late.

(He moves away from her.)

Eva: Have pity. Have pity on him.

Ox *(turning around)***:** It will be too late. *(Exit.)*

(Enter Eva. She comes downstage, distraught and exhausted.)

Eva: My God! What shall I do? What will become of me? He'll kill him! Ah! I feel faint. I can't do anything more. I think I'm dying. *(Calling)* George! George! George!

(Her voice trails away and she falls unconscious. At this point, behind the rocks upstage and on the sides, the wild inhabitants of this subterranean region reappear. They advance cautiously. One of them, who is their leader, guides them to center stage, where the unconscious young woman

is lying. They approach her and watch her with the keenest surprise. They bend over her. The leader kneels, lifts her head, lets down her hair, touches her face and hands, then listens to see whether she is still breathing. He looks around, signals to his companions to move aside, then lifts her up and is about to carry her off. Eva *regains consciousness, notices the monsters all around her, and utters a cry of horror.)*

Eva: Oh!

(Eva manages to break free and is about to run away when the leader seizes her again.)

Eva *(struggling)*: Help!

(The leader picks her up in his arms and rushes upstage.)

(Enter George, *running in from stage left.)*

George: Those cries! *(noticing Eva in the hands of the natives)* Eva!

Eva: Help! Help!

George: I'll save you, Eva. I'll save you or die with you!

(He rushes at the leader, but the others seize him and throw him to the ground.)

(Enter Dr. Ox, *stage right, then* Valdemar, Volsius, *and* Tartelet, *stage left.)*

Tartelet: Ah! My God!

Valdemar: Those horrible monsters!

Ox *(coldly)*: They're doomed!

(The natives turn toward them, then grip George *and* Eva *by the throat.)*

Eva and George: Ah!

George: Save her! Save Eva!

Tartelet: Let's run!

Volsius: Silence! *(He seizes the violin that* Tartelet *is carrying.)*

Ox: But her . . . Eva.

Volsius: Stand still, everyone!

(From the violin he produces sounds of a strange intensity. The natives stop, listen, and seem fascinated. Volsius *continues to play. The leader has released his grip on* Eva. *He slowly approaches* Volsius, *listening intently. He listens more closely. He brings his head up to the instrument. His companions also creep closer, as if chained to the bow.* Volsius *goes offstage again, followed by the natives, while the sound of the violin is still heard in the distance.)*

George *(runs to* Eva *and takes her in his arms)*: Ah! Eva! My dear Eva!

Eva: Let's get away from this cursed place. Take me away. Take me away, please.

Valdemar: Ah yes. Let's get away from here!

Tartelet: Ah! That Master Lidenbrok. I would never have played like that.

Valdemar: My friend, my dear friend, listen to me. Let's get out of here.

George: Yes, yes, they're right. Let's go back the way we came. Eva, I want to take you far away from here. I don't want to expose you to any more such dangers. Let's go.

Ox: Go? When at any moment the obstacle that lies between us and our goal may disappear?

George: What did you say?

Eva: Don't listen to that man, George. Don't listen to him.

(A rumbling is heard.)

Ox: Wait a minute. Listen, look. The ground is opening up at last. Look! Look, George Hatteras. This is the first step up on your road to fame and glory. It's the first step through the impossible!

—SCENE 5—

THE CENTRAL FIRE

The center of the earth. Everywhere there are flames,[25] showers of sparks, incandescent lava flowing in all directions. Torrents of liquid metal, molten silver and gold. Ox, George, Eva, Tartelet, *and* Valdemar *stand watching the spectacle.*

Ox: Well, now do you believe in the power I've given you? And do you promise to follow me from now on?

George: Everywhere, doctor, wherever you want to take me.

Eva *(aside)*: I've lost him!

George *(He has run through the theater, looking distractedly at everything)*: Yes, yes. This is really the incandescent center of the earth. There's fire everywhere, everywhere. I feel enveloped by it, but not consumed. I take deep breaths of it. And what a new life has come over me! What an irresistible strength! Fire is the soul of nature, the universal life. It makes my blood a thousand times hotter. It boils in my head and flows through my veins like torrents of lava.

Ox *(sarcastically)*: Good, good!

George: It electrifies my soul. It reveals to my wondering eyes mysteries unknown to man.

Ox *(to* Eva, *pointing to* George*)*: Listen to him. Look at him.

George: No, you are no longer empty and fictional beings, you marvellous inhabitants of fire. Come, phoenix, will-o'-the-wisp, salamanders, show yourselves. I'll shout throughout the world the news that you really exist, for I will have seen you. I see you. I see you!

(The phoenixes, will-o'-the-wisps, and salamanders appear.)

(BALLET[26])

(Toward the end of the ballet, Ox *brings* George *back to center stage.)*

Ox: Son of Hatteras! You have surpassed Professor Lidenbrok. Come now and outshine the glory of Captain Nemo!

(They disappear in the midst of the final dance.)

END OF ACT I

Cover sheet of a quadrille that was not in the play but was written because the play was such a success. The music of the play itself (the ballet) was lost, and this quadrille is the only surviving music connected with the play.

Act II
The Bottom of the Sea

─SCENE 1─

THE HARBOR
AT GOA

A square in Goa,[1] on the waterfront. To the right, the city appears in the form of an amphitheatre, with mosques, Hindu houses, and tree-shaded villas. To the left, a hotel with a tent and verandah, and to the right of this a jeweller's shop. In the background can be seen part of the harbor, with ships, fishing boats, and in the distance an ocean-going vessel about to leave under half-sail, flying the British flag. An Englishman, Captain Anderson,[2] *an* Officer, *a* jeweller, Hindus, porters, *and* sailors *mingle with a crowd of men and children. The crowd moves back and forth over the square, which is closed off at the end by a balustrade that forms a dock on the harbor. It is broad daylight.*

First Hindu: Well, has the terrible monster appeared again?

Jeweller: Not yet, but if it does, I wouldn't give a sequin[3] for all the ships in Goa harbor.

First Hindu: The Indian ocean is definitely not safe any more. I feel sorry for any ships sailing near our shores.

Voices *(in the crowd)*: There it is! There it is!

First Hindu: No, no, that's only the reflection of the sun on the horizon.

(The excited crowd rushes to the side of the square nearest the harbor.)

Jeweller: That terrible creature will make a lot of trouble for me. Ships won't dare come into Goa harbor any more. No more ships, no more travelers. Then what will happen to our business in jewellery and precious stones?

The Englishman *(to* Captain Anderson*)*: This sea monster is throwing a good many people into a panic, isn't it, captain?

The Officer: But wait a minute. Is it really a sea monster?

Anderson: What else could it be? Many sailors have seen it, and several ships that it attacked just barely escaped. It may even be responsible for the disappearance of a number of ships that have been lost without a trace.

The Officer: Oh, I don't deny that there have been catastrophes due to the presence of a powerful creature that has been appearing on the surface of the ocean for the past several years. One day it's in the Atlantic, another day in the Indian Ocean. It seems to have a prodigious ability to move from place to place.[4]

Anderson: It's a real danger to navigation. But I have business to discuss with some passengers over there. Will you excuse me, please?

The Officer: By all means, captain, by all means.

(Exit Anderson.)

(Enter Valdemar, coming out of the inn.)

Valdemar: Bon voyage, gentlemen. So now they're planning to visit the bottom of the sea. Well, I won't follow them. I went with them to the center of the earth. Fine! And I came back, which is even better! But now I've had enough. I didn't even find anything there, either in the fire or in the ground. The only thing I brought back was this *(taking a pebble from his pocket)*—this stone that hit me in the back. It's cluttering up my pocket for no good reason. I'm not going to carry it around any longer.

(He throws it onto the ground, accidentally hitting the foot of the jeweller as he comes out of his shop.)

The Jeweller: Ouch! What's this?

Valdemar: Excuse me, sir. It's a stone that I dropped.

The Jeweller *(annoyed)*: A stone, sir, a stone?

Valdemar: Yes. Look. It's a rather unusual stone, in fact. I brought it back from the center of the earth.

(Shows it to him.)

The Jeweller: From the center of the earth, did you say? *(examining the stone, aside)* But . . . No, I'm not mistaken. This pebble . . . Can it really be? . . . It's a . . . Yes, it's a precious stone.

Valdemar: A precious stone! If you think it's worth anything, what would you give me for it?

The Jeweller: I'd give you . . . I'd give you . . . two hundred sequins. How does that sound?

Valdemar *(with a surprised laugh)*: Two hundred sequins for that? Ha!

The Jeweller: Will you take it?

Valdemar *(laughing)*: You're making fun of me. Come, now. This stone? Two hundred sequins?

The Jeweller *(aside)*: He knows what it's worth. *(Aloud)* All right, then. My offer is . . .

Valdemar: Is a joke.

The Jeweller: That's right. Just a little joke.

Valdemar: That's what I said.

The Jeweller: Seriously, though, I'll give you ten thousand sequins for it.

Valdemar *(angrily)*: Ten thousand! Ah! Now you're really making fun of me sir, and I won't stand for it.

The Jeweller: Forgive me, your lordship, forgive me. Don't be angry. I see that you know perfectly well what your rough diamond is worth, and I am prepared to give you. . . .

Valdemar *(taking back the diamond)*: What did you say? My what?

The Jeweller: Your rough diamond.

Valdemar *(very agitated)*: My diamond. My rough diamond. It's a diamond, and still in the rough. All right, now. Let's understand each other. You're telling me that this is really a diamond?

The Jeweller: You mean you didn't know?

Valdemar: I hadn't the faintest idea.

The Jeweller (*in a loud voice*): He didn't know!

Valdemar: You're the one who told me just now. (*Shakes his hand.*) Thank you, thank you. You're an honest jeweller. It's a diamond! A diamond that you will buy for. . . .

The Jeweller: For five hundred thousand sequins. There! Do we have a deal?

Valdemar: It's a diamond! And what a size! A diamond that I've been offered five hundred thousand sequins for. That means it must be worth a million, at least. (*He dances.*) Tra deri dera deri deri dera.

The Jeweller: Have you decided not to sell it?

Valdemar: Oh I'll sell it, all right. I'll sell it in Europe, in France.

The Jeweller: In France!

Valdemar: My fortune will be made. And what a fortune! Ah! My dear little Babichok, my faithful fiancée, waiting for me back there, with cousin Finderup. Now I'll marry you, with cousin. . . . I'll marry you right away, by telegram. You'll be so happy! You can stop worrying that I'll be poor. And cousin Finderup. How delighted he will be! I'm rich! Rich! Rich! (*He dances.*) Tra deri dera deri dera dera. If Tartelet could see me now. And with my toes pointing out. Ah! What joy! What happiness!

The Jeweller (*aside*): He's going out of his mind!

Valdemar: My friend, is there a telegraph office in this town?

The Jeweller: Yes, and it has a line to Europe.

Valdemar: I can send a message, then?

The Jeweller: Of course.

Valdemar: And if I paid ten times, or a hundred times the price of the message, would I get an answer right away?

The Jeweller: Very likely.

Valdemar: Ah! Babichok! Dear little Babichok! I'm a millionaire! I'm a millionaire seventeen times over. You'll have carriages and castles and an Indian cashmere shawl. *(To the jeweller)* There must be Indian cashmere shawls in India?

The Jeweller: Splendid ones. They come from Paris.

Valdemar: I'll buy nine. The telegraph office. Where's the telegraph office?

The Jeweller *(aside)*: He's going crazy!

(Enter Anderson.)

Valdemar *(to Anderson)*: Excuse me, sir, where's the telegraph office?

Anderson: Over there, to the right.

Valdemar: Thank you, sir. I'm going to send a telegram to Babichok, sir, to tell her about my fortune.

(He runs out.)

The Jeweller: I missed out on a wonderful deal.

(He goes back into his shop.)

(Enter Dr. Ox, coming out of the hotel, followed by George, Tartelet, and Eva.)

Ox: Well, sir, is everything ready for us to come on board your ship?

Anderson: Yes, sir.

George *(excitedly)*: We're about to leave, any minute now. We'll reach the open sea, and when we're there, doctor. . . . Ah!

Ox *(in a low voice)*: Silence!

Anderson: My ship makes excellent time, gentlemen, and I have no doubt that within six weeks I can land you at Valparaiso.[5]

George: At Valparaiso! Us? Ah!

Eva *(looking at him nervously)*: George!

Ox: We will not be getting off your ship at Valparaiso, sir.

Anderson: But gentlemen, I am going directly from Goa to the coast of South America, and unless you want to get off in mid-ocean. . . .

Ox: Who knows? In mid-ocean? Perhaps.

George: In mid-ocean! Yes, that's the route we must take, diving through the water, down to the depths of the abyss.

Eva: George, you're terrifying me.

George *(coming out of his reverie)*: Eva, my dear Eva, don't worry. You won't have to face these dangers. I don't want you to.

Eva: I'll never be separated from you!

Anderson *(aside)*: I seem to have some peculiar passengers here.

Tartelet *(who has been mingling with the crowd, now comes back onstage)*: What are these good people saying? They claim there's a sea monster swimming about in their harbor.

Ox *(laughing)*: A monster?

Anderson: Don't laugh, gentlemen. There really has been a dreadful creature traveling through the waters of the Indian Ocean for the past month.

George: Good!

Anderson: What did you say?

George: We'll do battle with it, captain.

Ox: It's some mythical octopus,[6] some legendary Kraken.[7]

Anderson: No, it's a kind of whale, a phosphorescent monster about two hundred and fifty feet long. It creates a frightful eddy as it goes, and leaves a dazzling white wake behind it.

Shouts from the crowd: There it is! There it is!

Anderson: They must have caught sight of it just now.

George: Come on. Let's run!

(*He goes back upstage with* Ox *and* Anderson. *All three cross the dock at the back of the stage, amongst the crowd.*)

Tartelet: Ah! Poor Mr. George gets more and more excited all the time. Dr. Ox's control over him, with its incomprehensible power, is only too clearly justified. Now we're left to fend for ourselves. (*Looking around*) By the way, what's become of young Valdemar? Where can he be?

(Eva *goes back upstage and rejoins* George.)

(*Enter* Valdemar, *quickly, from the left.*)

Valdemar: Ah! Mr. Tartelet, my dear Mr. Tartelet.

Tartelet: What's the matter, young Valdemar?

Valdemar: The matter? What's the matter? I'm in such a state I can't talk. I can't say a word, Tartelet, I'm too flustered.

Tartelet: Yes! And when you're flustered, your toes point in. Look. Just look. Your feet!

Valdemar: This is no time to worry about such nonsense.

Tartelet (*hurt*): What's that? Nonsense, you say?

Valdemar: Later! I'll do whatever you want then. I'll take lessons from you at ten sous each, or a hundred francs, or a thousand francs.

Tartelet: He left his sanity behind in the central fire. His brain is cooked!

Valdemar: No, it isn't cooked, but it's boiling, it's boiling, it's boiling. Just think. That stone that hit me in the back.

Tartelet: What about it?

Valdemar: It's a diamond. A diamond! It's worth millions!

Tartelet: That's impossible.

Valdemar: I was offered five hundred thousand sequins for it, right here.

Tartelet: Five hundred thousand sequins? Here?

Valdemar: Yes. My dear Mr. Tartelet, I'm a millionaire. Or rather, we're millionaires.

Tartelet: We're millionaires, did you say? Did you say "we"? Ah, my friend. Ah, my good friend. You did say "we," didn't you?

Valdemar: Certainly. We're millionaires, Miss Babichok and I.

Tartelet: Ah! Miss Babi. . . . That's true, of course. Congratulations, Vladimir. Ah! Now she'll marry you.

Valdemar: Will she marry me! Twice over! So I've just sent a message to her in Copenhagen, telling her about my good luck and saying that I'm leaving shortly for Europe. I'm waiting now for her answer. Can you imagine what her answer will be?

Tartelet: Certainly I can imagine it. You'll be leaving us, then?

Valdemar: Yes, but I'm not a selfish person. I like you, Tartelet.

Tartelet: Thank you.

Valdemar: I'll brighten up the final years of your life, Tartelet. When you're old, you'll come and spend your last days in our house, in our castle. It will be a palace.

Tartelet: Old! But I'm old now, my friend, I'm old now.

Valdemar: Oh no, you're not old enough yet, Tartelet. It's your last— your very last days that I want to brighten up.

Tartelet *(aside)*: He's stupid, but he means well. *(Aloud)* Dear Matthew. Point your toes out, my friend, point your toes out!

Valdemar: Yes, professor, yes. Wait a minute! I'm rich! I'm entitled to point my toes in. See, this is how I want to walk from now on. *(He walks with his toes pointing in.)* I'll make it the fashion. I'm rich! And I'm really going to live up to my status from now on. This is the fashion, the real fashion.

(Enter Captain Anderson.)

(A boat large enough to hold seven or eight persons has come up to the dock.)

Anderson: Get in! Get in!

(George and Ox get in the boat.)

Tartelet: Goodbye, young Valdemar.

Valdemar: Goodbye, then, my dear professor.

(As Tartelet is about to embark, a telegram arrives.)

Employee: Mr. Valdemar? Telegram for Mr. Valdemar.

Valdemar: That's me! That's me! It's an answer from my darling Babichok.

Tartelet: What does she say?

Valdemar *(reads)*: "Dear Valdemar. Be happy. . . ." *(Speaks)* Oh yes, I am, I am! *(Reads)* ". . . without me. I have just married. . . ."

Tartelet: What did you say?

Valdemar *(reads)*: "Without me, I have just married. . . ." *(Speaks)* I don't understand.

Tartelet: Oh come now!

Anderson: Come along, gentlemen, come along!

Tartelet: We're coming.

Valdemar *(angrily)*: That hussy! Ah! I'll never see her again.

Tartelet: Take my advice, Valdemar. Forget that cheating woman and come with us.

Valdemar: Well, all right. I'll come. And she'll see, now that she's lost me, what a hero she's lost.

Anderson: Come along, gentlemen, come along.

(They both get in the boat.)

(The scene changes.)

–SCENE 2–

THE PLATFORM OF THE *NAUTILUS*

A moonlit night at sea.

Ox *(standing alone on the platform)*: Here it is, under my feet, the dreadful monster that spread terror among the people of Goa. It's Captain Nemo's submarine, the man whose fame my rival, my enemy, hopes to surpass. Be patient, George, be patient. I shall keep all my promises. I shall make your fondest dreams come true. And you will not have to pay for my services. She will pay! She whose image is constantly before my eyes, whose memory fills my entire soul. Eva! Eva! She is there, close to him. They were thrown onto this platform, just as I was, by the shock when the two vessels collided. Let me go and find her. Let me finish my work.

(He kicks the hull of the ship and an opening appears, through which he descends. The Nautilus *disappears, then reappears on stage. It opens slightly to reveal the interior chamber.)*

7.ᵉ Tableau.

La plate-forme du Nautilus.

La nuit en pleine mer et par un clair de lune.

——— Scène unique ———
Ox, seul, debout sur la plate-forme.

Il est là, sous mes pieds, ce redoutable monstre, qui jetait l'épouvante parmi les habitants de Goa. C'est le navire sous-marin du Capitaine Nemo, dont mon rival, mon ennemi, aspire à éclipser la renommée ! Patience, Georges, patience !... je tiendrai toutes mes promesses, je comblerai tes souhaits les plus ardents et ce ne sera pas à toi que je demanderai le prix des services rendus !... C'est à elle !... à elle, dont l'image est sans cesse présente à mes regards dont la pensée emplit toute mon âme ! Eva! Eva !... Elle est là, près de lui, ils ont été ainsi que moi, recueillis ici, quand le choc des deux navires nous a jetés sur cette plate-forme ! Allons la retrouver, allons achever mon œuvre

---

This short scene, with Dr. Ox standing alone on the deck of the *Nautilus*, was omitted from the French edition published in 1981. It appears in this edition as Act II, Scene 2.

— SCENE 3 —

THE *NAUTILUS*

The interior of the Nautilus, *front cutaway view. An interior chamber, elegantly furnished, lighted by electricity. Sofas on either side. All the machinery is upstage. On the outside, the hull of the* Nautilus, *which is completely submerged, is in contact with the water, which covers it above the platform. Backstage, doors leading to the engine room.*

(*Enter* Eva, George, *and* Ox.)

George: What a strange, mysterious craft this is!

Ox: It can dive at will to the bottom of the ocean or sail on the surface. It travels without sails and without steam, powered by electricity alone.

George: And it's obviously armed with a formidable ram, because when our ship tried to block its way, it rushed forward violently and tore a large hole in the *Tranquebar's*[8] hull that nearly sent her to the bottom.

Eva: That was when we were taken on board here. But what can have happened to our two fellow passengers?

George: They probably stayed on board.

Eva: Or perhaps they were thrown into the sea.

Ox: In that case, they have nothing to fear. Thanks to my valuable discovery, they can live and breathe under water.

George: But what are we doing here? What ship is this, and who is its captain?

(*Enter* Volsius, *disguised as* Captain Nemo.)

Volsius: You are on board the *Nautilus*, and you are prisoners of Captain Nemo.

George, Eva: Captain Nemo!

Ox *(to* George*)***:** You wanted to make the acquaintance of this hero of the undersea world. Now you know him.

Volsius: Are you really sure that you know me, gentlemen?

George: We have known you for a long time, by your name and by your exploits.

Eva: We don't suppose you intend to treat us as enemies.

George: And hold us prisoner aboard your ship.

Volsius: When you are better acquainted with the *Nautilus*, you may not want to leave her.

All: Not leave her? Us?

Volsius: Life is a hundred times more peaceful and more independent on my ship than it is in your world. Here, you have no need to worry about storms at sea or persecution at the hands of man. Hurricanes may rage on the surface, but thirty feet down there is absolute calm. Whatever despots may rule on earth, my *Nautilus* goes down into the depths of the ocean and I can defy all the tyrannies of the world. Liberty[9] is still to be found, gentlemen, a hundred feet below the surface of the sea.

Ox: Liberty? Inside a prison?

George: That may be liberty for a misanthropist or a savage, but not for a civilized man.

Volsius: I reject that title, gentlemen. No, I am not what you call a civilized man. I have severed all ties with your society. I have left your earthly habitat forever. And I was in rather good company as I went into exile. God had just been banished from earth at that very moment—the "so-called God," as people say now.[10]

Ox *(sarcastically)***:** I see that Captain Nemo is a devout believer.

Volsius: Very devout,[11] and firmer in his beliefs than those whom I see displaying an atheism born of pride or fear.

Ox: Pride or fear, did you say?

Volsius: Yes, certainly. Most of those who claim to be atheists are either arrogant or afraid. If there were a God, say the arrogant ones, would a superior man like me, a man of genius, stagnate here unrecognized? The others, speaking out of fear, say there is no God.

All: Out of fear?

Volsius: Yes, gentlemen, fear. Examine the lives of these men. Dig into their past. Study their consciences. You will always find some dreary and mysterious reason, some dark memory, that makes them fear a supreme tribunal. They are afraid, I tell you. And why do they go around shouting and proclaiming everywhere that God does not exist? The reason is not so much a desire to convince others as the vain hope of convincing themselves.

Ox *(laughs)*: Ha ha! From the depths of the ocean, Captain Nemo wants to reawaken faith and reform our civilization.

Volsius: Ah, what a wonderful civilization it is! And on what an unshakable foundation this modern society rests, a society that steals from the disinherited of this world the hope of a better world to come. But if there is no life anywhere but on earth, if we have no expectation of any future punishment or reward, virtue is a fraud. Crime has only to find a way of skillfully evading the law. And should you happen to have a government headed by a few worthy and honest leaders who practice a gentle, bourgeois philosophy and are pleased to commute the sentences handed down by Justice, you will see the ranks of hardened criminals increase without letup. Since murder will be no more severely punished than theft, thieves will become murderers, and the murderers will say to themselves, "We can kill without fear; they won't kill us. We can cut throats without remorse; remorse is an empty word, since God does not exist."

George: What do you intend to do with us?

Eva: Please, sir, don't keep us here. None of us will betray your secret.

Volsius: Well, I'm a magnanimous person, and I'm willing to let my ship take you . . . wherever you want to go.

George: But we're on our way to conquer the impossible, through fire, through space.

Volsius: And through water, too, no doubt. Pour me a few drops of your precious potion, and I'll go with you, Dr. Ox.

Ox: Ah! You know . . . ?

Volsius: Your conversation reached me just now through the walls of the *Nautilus.* Yes, I know your name, learned doctor, and I know all about your wonderful discovery, just as I know who you are, George Hatteras.

George: George Hatteras, the son of a man who never retreated before any obstacle, and who went. . . .

Volsius: Who went to his death,[12] where you are in danger of going yourself.

George: Enough of your lessons, sir. I am not about to take lessons from you, even on board your ship.

Volsius (*sadly*)**:** You will take lessons, unfortunately, and more dreadful ones than I can teach you. You want to leave the *Nautilus* to run around at the bottom of the ocean. Very well, then, I'll go with you, as I said I would.

Ox: Even if I don't provide you with the means to live where the elements of life are not to be found?

Volsius: Even without that.

George: All right, then. Whenever you like, sir.

Volsius: Right now.

(*The* Nautilus *closes up and moves away through the water.*)

–SCENE 4–

UNDERWATER NAVIGATION

The open part of the Nautilus *gradually closes, then moves ahead so as to show the shape of the stern with its spinning propeller. The* Nautilus *goes off stage obliquely.*

–SCENE 5–

ON THE OCEAN FLOOR

The bottom of the sea. Enter Valdemar *stage right. Schools of fish swim around under his feet and disappear through the water.*

Valdemar: This is really and truly the bottom of the sea. I'm living, walking, and breathing under water, just like an ordinary herring. What a strange country! The roads are badly maintained, but certainly well watered. Not too much sun, either. *(Looking around.)* And my friends, what has become of them? I thought Tartelet dived in at the same time as I did. He must have been carried away by the current. *(Schools of fish swim by over his head.)* Ah! Fish! Frrr . . . Frrr . . . They're flying away, like birds. Good! There are some jellyfish. They look like colored parasols. But there are no ladies under them who can give me directions. *(While he is speaking, a large crab makes its way obliquely toward him. Suddenly he notices it.)* A crab! A crab! What an ugly creature. But it's coming after me! *(He tries to run away, dodging from side to side.)* But I don't know you. I don't know you. It will catch me sooner or later, the beast! Go lie down! *(At that moment an enormous shark appears in the water above him and swims down closer and closer to the bottom.)* And that fish! What a mouth! What teeth! A shark! It's a shark! Help! Help! Save me! *(In desperation, he goes in one direction, then another, but the crab is at his heels and the shark comes closer, opening* *its formidable jaws.)* Help! *(He starts to run, with the crab and shark in pursuit.)*

(The scene changes.)

— SCENE 6 —
AN UNDERWATER FOREST

Valdemar: Ouf! Those two horrible creatures are out of sight. Where am I now? A forest! I didn't expect to find a forest under water. *(He stops in front of an immense oyster.[13])* Well, well, an oyster. And what a fine oyster! A dozen of that size would make a nice appetizer for lunch. Maybe I'll have a taste. But no, this is August. There's no "R" in this month, so it can't be fresh. *(Just then a gigantic octopus appears.* Valdemar *notices it.)* Oh my goodness! What now? An octopus. A horrible octopus. What? It's chasing me, too. I'm done for! Where can I run? Where can I hide? Ah! The oyster! The hospitable oyster. *(Valdemar rushes toward the open oyster and crawls inside. The two halves suddenly close. The octopus disappears.)*

(Enter Tartelet. *He looks around carefully. From time to time he stops and calls out.)*

Tartelet *(shouts)*: Valdemar! Valdemar! *(He moves downstage.)* No one there. But I saw him sink at the same time as I did. There's no use calling and looking around. There's no one there. I've been looking for a long time, and I'm really tired. *(He sits on the large oyster in which* Valdemar *is hiding.)* Let's take a little rest. What has happened to my fellow passengers? Doctor Ox? I'm not worried about him, but what about Mr. George, and especially Miss Eva? *(As he is speaking, the oyster slowly begins to open.)* What a strange effect weariness has on me. The rock I'm sitting on seems to be rising. *(He feels himself being lifted by the upper half.)* Hey! What's going on underneath me? No, I'm not mistaken, it's really rising. It's moving. It's definitely rising. *(Trembling.)* Oh my goodness!

What's that? *(He presses down and the oyster closes again.)* There's a creature in there. It's rising. It's still rising.

Valdemar *(inside the oyster, which is partly open)*: Who is pressing down on my shell? Hey! You up there!

Tartelet *(trembling)*: Now it's talking. It's talking!

Valdemar *(opening the shell wider and putting his head out)*: Tartelet!

Tartelet: It knows my name. It's an oyster that I've met before.

Valdemar: It's me, Mr. Tartelet.

Tartelet: Valdemar!

Valdemar *(kneeling inside the oyster)*: Here I am, Mr. Tartelet.

Tartelet: It was you!

Valdemar: In person!

Tartelet: Inside an oyster?

Valdemar: Why yes. I was quite comfortable in there. I felt right at home. Oh, I'm so happy to see you again. Is everything all right, Mr. Tartelet?

Tartelet: Perfectly all right.

Valdemar: And what about Mr. George? And Mis Eva? And Dr. Ox?

Tartelet: I hope we'll see them again soon.

Valdemar: That's better. But I'd rather see them on terra firma, or, as we say in Copenhagen, on the calves' floor.[14]

Tartelet: Ah! What kind of floor did you say they call it in Copenhagen?

Valdemar: The calves' floor, Mr. Tartelet.

Tartelet: In our country, when we talk about dry land, we call it the cows' floor. But I was just thinking. . . . What were you doing in that seashell?

Valdemar: I was hiding from a crab.

Tartelet: From a crab?

Valdemar: And from a shark.

Tartelet: A shark?

Valdemar: And from a giant octopus.

Tartelet (*gesturing*)**:** An octopus? Ah, yes, an octopus.

Valdemar: All three of them were chasing me, and I can imagine what they had in mind.

Tartelet: What did they have in mind, Valdemar?

Valdemar: Well, you see, Tartelet, on dry land, people eat fish, but I think, at the bottom of the sea, fish eat people.

Tartelet: You're making me nervous, Valdemar.

Valdemar: Ah! I had a bad scare. I'd really like to get away from here and go back up to the surface.

Tartelet: We'll go back up, but first we have to find our fellow passengers.

Valdemar: Ah! If only that ungrateful Babichok hadn't married the traitor Finderup, I'd be in Copenhagen now. I'd be married and living in my own house. What am I saying? In my palace! And eating six meals a day.

Tartelet: Six meals?

Valdemar: Of course! I used to eat three when I was poor. The least I can do, now that I'm rich, is eat six or eight.

Tartelet: That's reasonable.

Valdemar: I can afford it.

(A tentacle of the octopus appears above the rock.)

Tartelet: Yes, indeed. And if your stomach can also afford it. . . .

(The tentacle waves back and forth above Valdemar's *head.)*

Valdemar: My stomach? Oh, I'm quite sure it can. . . . Hey! What's this I feel? *(The tentacle has wound itself around his waist.)* Help, Tartelet, help me! *(The tentacle drags him behind the rock.)* Tartelet! Tartelet!

Tartelet: Oh, good heavens! The poor fellow!

Valdemar *(reappears in the grip of the tentacle, which is waving him around)* Help! Help! It's choking me! Help!

Tartelet: What can I do? Help! Help!

*(*Tartelet *draws back at first, overcome by a powerful fear. Then he rushes at the octopus in order to pull* Valdemar *free. But another tentacle knocks him down, and he is unable to move.)*

(Enter Ox, George, Volsius, *and* Eva *from the back.* Volsius *and* George *rush at the monster.* Eva, *terrified, dashes toward* Tartelet, *who has stood up and now holds her.* Ox *joins his friends, who are attacking the octopus with their daggers. At this moment, several other octopuses appear and attack them. Everyone joins in the fight. Then the octopuses emit a blackish liquid which completely obscures the water. The combatants can be seen through a kind of heavy fog and eventually disappear completely.)*

— SCENE 7 —

THE CORAL REEF

The fog lifts and the stage represents coral caves.

(Enter Valdemar, Volsius, Tartelet, Ox, George, *and* Eva.*)*

Valdemar *(still only half conscious)***:** Where am I?

Eva: You're safe here.

George: You have nothing to fear now.

Valdemar: Really? Ah, sir! Ah, my friends!

Volsius: You're quite safe now.

Valdemar (*distraught and weeping*)**:** Yes, yes, quite safe. I want to get away. I want to get away.

Eva: You've had a bad fright, Mr. Valdemar.

Valdemar: Oh yes, miss. Yes, I've been frightened a great many times in my life. In fact, I think I can say without boasting that no one has ever been frightened more often than I have. But a fright like this one? Ah! Never, never! Please let me get away from here.

Volsius: But, as I told you before, here amongst these coral reefs, under so much pressure, you're safe from all sea monsters.

Valdemar: That may be, but I'd rather leave.

Volsius: There's nothing to keep you here now. We've reached the very bottom of the sea.

Eva: And this is the spot, no doubt, from which we'll be heading back up to dry land?

Ox: Back to dry land? Not yet.

George: Are there any more unknown wonders down here, any still unsolved mysteries?

Volsius: None, I guarantee you.

Ox: And I guarantee the very opposite. Anyone can come here and live, at least for a few moments. This is almost the possible. But let's go on farther and the impossible will rise up before your eyes, and the past, the irrevocable past itself, will spring up and take shape again before you.

All: The past?

Ox: Do you see those indistinct forms, those objects standing out vaguely, far off in the water?

(*Lines indicating vaguely the outlines of a submerged city appear in a confused way.*)

George: What's this?

Ox: Ask Captain Nemo. He'll tell you what it is. He's traveled through these waters many times.

Volsius: Here at one time was Atlantis, the immense continent described by Plato,[15] bigger than Africa and Asia combined. In a night and a day, it disappeared under the sea, as a result of some frightful cataclysm.

George: Atlantis?

Ox: Yes, Atlantis. This is where the famous Atlantean people lived, who subjugated almost the whole earth, who helped the Titans in their attempt to climb up to heaven and drive out the gods. Tell me, now, do you want to run away at the very moment when you're about to set foot on this continent, which no other human being will ever see again?

George: No, no. But these are only shapeless ruins.

Ox: They are the ruins of Makhimos,[16] one of the most famous capitals of Atlantis, which will revive and rise to the surface of the sea for you.

(The scene changes.)

– S C E N E   8 –

A T L A N T I S

The city square in Makhimos, capital of Atlantis, four or five thousand years B.C. The architecture combines Moorish, Arabic, and the style of Mexican burial caves. The water has entirely disappeared. Beautiful sunshine lights up the whole stage. Two Atlanteans, Ascalis[17] and Ammon,[18] are walking around among a crowd of people.

A Herald *(shouts)*: Glory to the gods, and may they inspire the people to raise a new king onto the throne of Atlantis.

All: Glory to the gods.

Ammon: Many days have gone by, and still we wait for a worthy successor to King Atlas.[19]

Ascalis: His only child is a daughter, Celena,[20] who cannot succeed him on the throne.

Ammon: Celena, the most beautiful woman in Atlantis, will not be queen until she has married the king whom we shall choose, and who, like this glorious sovereign, must brave the thunderbolts of Jupiter and climb up to heaven.

The Herald *(shouts)*: Glory to the gods. May they inspire the people to raise a new king onto the throne of Atlantis.

All: Glory to the gods!

(Enter Electra.[21])

All: The prophetess!

Ammon: What is Electra about to tell us? Has she consulted the oracles? Has she read the future?

Electra: This is the day, O people, when the throne, left vacant by the death of the greatest of kings, will finally be occupied.

All: Ah!

Ascalis: What mortal will be worthy to succeed him?

Electra: Listen, all of you. Atlas was vanquished by the Gods and fell when he supported the Titans in their revolt against heaven. But he whose coming is announced to us is no mere mortal. I have consulted the entrails of the sacrificial victims and drunk the intoxicating potion of the laurel bush. When I took my place on the prophetic tripod of the sibyls,[22] a strange man, born in a far-off country and endowed with supernatural powers, appeared to me.

Ammon: What man is that?

Ascalis: What mystery did he reveal? Tell us.

All: Yes, tell us.

Electra: Wait. He who calls himself the messenger of destiny will announce it himself.

Ascalis: Let him come, then.

All: Let him come.

Electra: Here he is.

(Enter Ox.)

Ammon: Who are you, O stranger?

Ox: I am the messenger of him whom your prophecies have foretold, of him who is to reign over Atlantis.

Ascalis: Is our race so inferior that no man worthy of the throne can be found among us?

Ox: When you know what prodigious feats the one whom I represent has performed in order to reach you, he will be your unanimous choice.

Ammon: Is this a God, then, that you are bringing us?

Ox: It is a man, one whose courage has raised him above all the rest of humanity. Neither fire, nor water, nor terrestrial abysses hold any secrets for him. Compared to this daring man, what are the outstanding heroes of your history? Tell me, is there a single one of them who can be compared to him?

All: No, no.

Electra: Let him come, and by popular acclamation he will be raised to a position of supreme power. And he will be the fortunate husband of Celena.

Ox: Celena?

Electra: The wonder of Atlantis, the incomparable daughter of King Atlas.

Ox: Let it be done as you say. He who comes after me will be the worthy husband of your king's daughter.

(Enter George *and* Eva.*)*

Ox: Here is the man you are waiting for.

All: All hail! All hail!

George: What do they want of me?

Ox: They have heard from me of the prodigious feats you have accomplished, and their admiration calls you to the throne of Atlantis.

Eva: What are you saying?

George: Who? Me? I'm going to be . . . ?

Ox: You're going to be king.

All: Yes, yes!

Eva: Oh God!

George: You heard what he said. You heard him, Eva, you heard him. King of this powerful nation, conquered long ago. What an honor! What glory! What a triumph!

Eva *(aside)*: Ah! So that's why he brought him here. This is the last attack on his sanity. *(Aloud)* George, listen to me. Listen to my voice. Reject this false royalty.

George: False, did you say, when I am the ruler of a whole nation that has been restored to life for me? For me, who will unite, from this moment on, the marvellous memories of antiquity and the glorious discoveries of the present. What power can be compared to mine? King of this continent, which extends from the ancient world to the present. I'm king! I'm king!

Ox: And this immense population will bow before him who has done what no man had ever done before.

George *(raving)*: Yes! Yes! Ah! It has come at last, the glory I have longed for, the supremacy I have so ardently dreamed of. I, the son of Hatteras, I am king of Atlantis!

Eva: Don't let your pride lead you on. Close your ears to these cursed temptations.

All: All hail! All hail!

George: Listen. Don't you hear the people cheering me?

Eva: These people.... Are you forgetting that they are only an empty recollection of the past? That this country is a short-lived empire? That this royalty is a mirage in which your imagination is wandering aimlessly about? George, my darling George, I'm pleading with you. Take pity on my tears.

George: Your tears! Yes, yes, you're crying, Eva. Ah! I don't want you to cry. Really, I don't want you to cry.

Eva: Listen to me, then. Listen carefully.

George: Go on. Go on.

Eva: George, you are walking down a fatal slope that leads to delirium, to madness!

George: Delirium, did you say? Madness?

Eva: Yes, yes. Take my word for it. Have I ever deceived you?

George: Yes, I believe in you, and I want . . . I want to struggle. Speak to me, Eva, speak to me.

Eva *(overjoyed)*: Ah! Our love will save him! Take courage, George, take courage! Fight on! I fall at your knees. I am your friend, your sister, your fiancée.

George: Wait, wait. Light is dispelling the darkness. Truth will shine before my eyes.

Eva: And you will be saved! You will be saved, George.

Ox: *(aside)*: Saved! *(Aloud)* Glory to your sovereign!

All: Glory to him! Glory to our king!

George *(in a loud voice)*: Ah! You heard him! King! I really am king!

Electra: Come to the palace that Makhimos has erected for its sovereigns. When you return to this spot, all the assembled multitudes will crown you with their acclaim.

Eva: No, no. Don't desert me.

All: Glory to him! Glory to him!

George: Come, all of you.

(Exit all except Eva *and* Ox.)

Eva *(uttering a final cry)*: Alas! It's all over!

(She is about to rush after George, *but* Ox *motions to her, and she stops.)*

Ox: One more outburst like that, one more attack on his sanity, and he will be completely demented, his madness will be incurable.

Eva: Yes, this is where your treachery has brought him, to destroy him.

Ox: Not to destroy him, but to win you, Eva.

Eva: To win me?

Ox: His fate is in my hands, is it not?

Eva: What does that matter?

Ox: You no longer tremble for him, then?

Eva: No!

Ox: Nor for yourself?

Eva: No!

Ox: What are you waiting for, then? What do you still hope for?

Eva: I'm waiting for a greater power to intervene on his behalf. I'm waiting for his love to save him, or for him to die!

Ox: If he dies, at least I will have separated you.

Eva: There you are wrong. If he dies, I'll die with him.

Ox: You would die for this man who has forgotten you, who has never loved you?

Eva: Never loved me, did you say?

Ox: Never! Because he doesn't seek his life's happiness in you, but elsewhere. He only had to reach out his hand and grasp that happiness, but he scorned your love in order to realize his wild dreams.

Eva: Even if George no longer loved me, I would still love him. I'll always love him, always, do you hear?

(Enter Volsius.)

Ox *(beside himself)*: Be quiet! Be quiet! I warn you, don't drive me to despair. Stop tormenting my soul.

Volsius: But you yourself are trying to torment her soul, are you not?

Ox: Who dares to speak to me in that tone?

Volsius *(approaching)*: I do.

Ox: We're not aboard your vessel now, Captain Nemo, and you're not all-powerful here. Be careful.

Volsius: I warn you, sir, that I am not easily intimidated.

Ox: That makes no difference to me. And who asked you to become involved?

Eva: I did.

Volsius *(to Eva)*: And your request will not go unanswered.

Ox: Captain Nemo wants to fight with me.

Volsius: I want to wrest from your hands someone whom your cursed science would push from the intermittent delirium that now obsesses him into a state of final and terrible madness. That is what I want, and I will find in you yourself a weapon to use against you.

Ox: A weapon? In me? A weapon to use against me?

Volsius: You love this young woman, and the love that eats at your soul will be your punishment. It will do battle for us.

Ox: My love!

Volsius: And God said to the serpent, "The woman shall crush thy head beneath her heel." And I say to you that this woman's disdain will break your pride. This woman will crush your heart beneath her scorn and her hatred.

Ox: We'll see about that.

Volsius: Yes, we'll see.

(The sound of cheering outside.)

Ox: Meanwhile. . . . Listen. It's Hatteras's people cheering him, leading him toward the throne where glory and love await him.

Eva: Love!

Ox: Yes, yes, the most beautiful of the daughters of this country, the descendent of King Atlas, is intended for him.

Eva: Oh my God!

Ox: And this time he will not only forget you; he will betray you. Your George will love someone else.

Eva: No, no, that's impossible!

(Enter a great procession composed of the entire royal court of Atlantis, with warriors and lords surrounding the new king. George, clothed in royal robes, is about to take his place on the uppermost steps of the stairway rising at the back, after the procession has passed by to the sound of music and the cheers of the people.)

(Enter George, Electra, Ammon, Ascalis, Celena, Atlanteans, Lords, officers, soldiers, people, slaves.)

All: All hail! All hail!

George: People of Atlantis, I accept the crown of this immense kingdom, and its power will not diminish during the reign of Hatteras.

All: Long live Hatteras!

(Enter Princess Celena *in the procession.* Electra *walks toward the princess and leads her to the foot of the stairs on which* George *sits enthroned.)*

Electra: And now, O king, here is the Princess Celena, who, through you, will become our queen.

All: Hail, Celena!

(The princess is about to take her place beside George.*)*

Eva *(rushing forward)*: His wife! No, no! That's impossible! George! George! Have you forgotten the past, your promises, our love? George, do you want me to die at your feet?

George *(whispers)*: Eva, you will share my throne and my power.

Eva: But this throne is ephemeral, this power is a figment of your imagination.

George: What did you say?

Eva: Come back to reality.

Ox: Reality, George Hatteras, is everything you see, everything that is around you. It is your glory, which is already great and will soon be even more dazzling.

George: Speak. Explain yourself.

Eva: Don't listen to him, George. Don't listen to him.

Ox: I promised your new subjects, in your name, that the work begun by Atlas would be completed by you.

Eva: You dare to say this?

Ox: I say . . . I say to the people of Atlantis that your king will carry out the great project that has been interrupted. Atlas, it is said, was struck down by a thunderbolt. But your king will answer Jupiter with another thunderbolt, newly created by the genius of man. Carried by that same thunderbolt, launched into space by bronze or steel, he will traverse the infinite and rise to celestial light.

George *(wild with delight)*: Indeed he shall!

Eva: Ah! All is lost!

All: Glory to him! Glory to the son of Hatteras!

Volsius: Don't despair. This dream will soon disappear, and with reality his sanity will return, but perhaps for the last time.

George: After the bowels of the earth and the depths of the ocean will come space, the infinite, Heaven!

(Horsemen bring in a horse, which George *mounts, and they are raised up on a richly carpeted shield.)*

All: All hail! All hail!

(Curtain)

END OF ACT II

Act III
The Planet Altor

─ S C E N E 1 ─

T H E G U N C L U B

A room at the Gun Club in the United States, specially decorated with panoplies. Columns made up of cannons are supported by mortars. On the walls hang strings of bombs, necklaces of missiles, garlands of shells. On the right, Barbicane,[1] the club president, is sitting at his desk, on which there is an array of revolvers which he uses as a bell to restore order by firing shots in the air from time to time. Maston[2] and other club members occupy the benches downstage. It is daytime. As the curtain rises, the uproar in the assembly is at its peak.

First Group: Yes! Yes! Yes!

Second Group: No! No! No!

Barbicane: My dear colleagues. . . .

First Group: To hell with the motion!

Second Group: And with the people who moved it.

Barbicane: A little silence, if you please!

First Group: Yes! Yes! Yes!

Second Group: No! No! No!

(Barbicane *fires a revolver.*)

An Usher: Silence, gentlemen.

Maston: Let President Barbicane speak. What a president, gentlemen, what a president!

Barbicane: Gentlemen, the question is very simple, and it would have been settled already if you had not been making so much noise.

First Member: But here at the Gun Club, we are all artillerymen.

Maston: And what artillerymen, gentlemen! Artillerymen and Americans!

First Member: That means we are doubly entitled to make a noise.

First Group: Yes! Yes! Yes!

Second Group: No! No! No!

Barbicane: Gentlemen, I do not believe I have gone too far. . . .

First Member: An artilleryman could never go too far.

Maston: No farther than his projectile will carry.

Barbicane: Gentlemen!

First Group: Yes! Yes! Yes!

Second Group: No! No! No!

(Barbicane *fires his revolver.*)

The Usher: Silence, gentlemen!

(Silence is restored.)

Barbicane: Gentlemen, you remember the circumstances under which our original experiment was carried out. A gigantic cannon, a Columbiad,[3] was set up on the ground in Florida.[4] A projectile was placed in it, in which three travellers took their places: my friend Captain Nicholl.[5] . . .

Maston: What a captain, gentlemen, what a captain!

Barbicane: Our friend Ardan, the French interpreter. . . .

Maston: What a Frenchman, gentlemen, what a Frenchman!

Barbicane: And myself, your president.

Maston: What a president!

Barbicane: But because it was not aimed accurately, we did not reach our objective. Our projectile merely circled the Moon, then came back and fell into the Pacific Ocean. Now, the Columbiad is still there. All we have to do is reload it. Should we resume the experiment and send a second projectile toward the Moon—and make sure we reach it this time?

First Group: Yes! Yes! Yes!

Second Group: No! No! No!

Barbicane: I believe I understood you to say yes?

Second Group: No! No! No!

Barbicane: Or maybe it was no.

First Group: Yes! Yes! Yes!

Both Groups Together: No! No! No! Yes! Yes! Yes!

(*General uproar.* Barbicane *fires his revolver.*)

The Usher: Silence, gentlemen!

Maston: For the honor of the club, the experiment must be repeated.

All: Call the question!

Maston (*to his neighbor*): I forbid you to vote against the motion!

First Member: I forbid you to vote for it.

Maston (*angrily*): Will you listen to reason?

First Member: How can I listen to reason when you are being so unreasonable?

Maston: Sir!

First Member: Sir!

Barbicane: Gentlemen, order, please! We are not in parliament here, for God's sake!

First Member: Name your weapon.

Maston: Name yours.

First Member: A repeating rifle.

Maston: A revolver.

First Member: In an hour!

Maston: Right now!

Barbicane: Gentlemen!

First Member: At fifteen paces.

Maston: At ten paces.

First Member: At five paces.

Maston: At no paces at all.

First Member: Let's go outside.

Maston: No, let's fight here.

First Group: Yes! Yes! Yes!

Second Group: No! No! No!

(Maston *and the club member rush at one another with a shout.*)

Barbicane: Separate them!

First Group: Come on, hurrah for Maston!

Second Group: Come on, down with Maston!

(*The members of the club rush to back their supporters. President* Barbicane *fires his revolver several times, to no effect. The uproar is at its peak.*)

The Usher: Silence, gentlemen!

(*Enter an usher of the Gun Club in the midst of the confusion. He hands a letter to the president.*)

Barbicane: The reason I have made this proposal to you is that I have just received this letter from the famous Dr. Ox.

All: The famous Dr. Ox!

Maston: What a doctor, gentlemen, what a doctor!

A Member: And what does the letter say?

All: Let's hear it, let's hear it.

Barbicane *(reading)*: "Distinguished president: Dr. Ox and his young colleague, George Hatteras, have just arrived in this city, and request an opportunity to make a proposal to the members of the Gun Club that will be of keen interest[6] to them."

Maston: A proposal?

Barbicane: I think we should hear it. Is Dr. Ox here?

The Usher: He is ready to appear before the members of the Gun Club.

Barbicane (then everyone): Show him in.

(Enter Ox and George.)

Barbicane: Welcome, distinguished Dr. Ox.

Maston: Three cheers for Dr. Ox.

All: Three cheers for Dr. Ox!

Ox: First of all, gentlemen, allow me to introduce my young colleague, George Hatteras, son of the glorious captain of that name.

Maston: Three cheers for the son of Captain Hatteras!

All: Hip, hip, hurrah!

George: Before you honor me with your acclamations, gentlemen, let me tell you what I have done and what else I want to accomplish.

All: Tell us!

Ox: You will learn soon enough what he has done. As for what he wants to undertake, he has come to ask for your help with that task.

George: Yes, my ambition is to leave this earth, which I have explored to its deepest recesses. What I want now is to set foot in the infinite, outside our globe altogether.

Barbicane: You can count on our support.

Ox: Here is the proposal we have come to make to you.

Maston (*shouting*)**:** Silence, gentlemen, silence.

Barbicane: But Mr. Maston, no one is speaking except you.

Maston: Really? In that case, I'm speaking to myself.

Ox: Gentlemen, after your first experiment, which raised the glory of America to the skies, you decided not to destroy the giant Columbiad, whose projectile rose more than a hundred thousand leagues into the air. We ask you to repeat the experiment, but to correct the aim this time, so as not to miss the target.

(Whispers)

George: Well, gentlemen, do you agree? Will you allow me, on your behalf, to conquer this satellite of the earth, which even the most daring among us has only gone round in orbit? Will you let me finally complete the third stage of my journey through the impossible?

All: Yes! Yes!

Ox: By accepting our proposal, gentlemen, you will have proved once more that nothing in this world is impossible.

Maston: Impossible is not an American word.

George: Nor English either.

(Enter Volsius, *disguised as* Ardan.*)*

Volsius: Nor French either, gentlemen.

Maston: Ardan! Our friend Ardan!

All: Hurrah for Ardan!

Barbicane: My worthy friend!

(He has left his presidential desk, and now comes to shake hands with Ardan, *who is surrounded by the members of the club.)*

Volsius: Yes, my friends, it is I, Michel Ardan. I have arrived just now on the *Labrador*. I heard that the Gun Club was holding a meeting, and I have made this my first visit.

Maston: What a man! Even if he is a Frenchman.

Barbicane: The French are a great people, gentlemen. There's only one thing they need to make them the greatest people in the world.

Maston: Yes, only one.

Volsius: And that is . . . ?

Maston: They need to be Americans.

Volsius: Thank you!

Barbicane: My dear friend, you come at an opportune time. Our first experiment has had its imitators.

Volsius: Imitators! Do you mean to say that there are madmen under the dome of Heaven who are even madder than we are?

Maston: Madmen?

Ox: That doesn't sound to me like the language of the daring Ardan.

Volsius: What did you say, sir?

Barbicane: This is Dr. Ox, and this is his young colleague, George Hatteras.

George: Who is determined, sir, to take possession of a world that has eluded you.

Volsius: What do you mean, young man? Don't stand on ceremony. The Moon belongs to the first person who occupies it. What then? What will you do with the Moon?

George: We will. . . .

Maston: Present it to the United States. It will be one more state for the Union.

All: Yes! Yes!

Volsius: The Moon? Why, it's a worn-out star, finished, out of date, even a little ridiculous. She's had her day, that old Astarte,[7] the mummified sister of the radiant Apollo.[8] People will laugh at your journey, and when you come back they'll shout, "So you saw the Moon, my lad, did you?"

Ox: Is this really the famous Ardan speaking like this?

Volsius: And the day will come when everyone will go to the Moon, and even farther. Aerial trains will ply the airways. Instead of railway cars running on rails, projectiles will be attached together and launched into space. Trains bound for all the planets. An express for Mercury, Uranus, and Neptune. But the Moon! Bah! The Moon! It will soon be nothing but a suburb of the earth, where people will go to spend Sunday, as Parisians go to Chatou or Vésinet.[9]

Maston: Well said, Ardan my friend.

Volsius: Take my advice, George Hatteras. Give up this plan and go quietly back home.

George: You mean give up the idea of leaving the earth?

Volsius: Oh, you'll leave it soon enough, my dear fellow.

Ox: Ah! You think, Mr. Ardan, that the Moon is not worth exploring?

Volsius: That is my opinion, Dr. Ox.

Ox: Well then, you have made a convert.

George: Can that be possible?

Ox: Yes! Yes! We must forget about that humble planet, that cold satellite of the earth. We must start out toward a nobler and more distant goal.

Volsius and All: What is he saying?

George: Towards the Sun, then.

Ox: Farther yet.

George: Jupiter? Uranus?

Ox: Still farther! Farther, outside our solar system.

George (*in great excitement*): Ah! I understand, doctor. Yes! Yes! To lose oneself in the infinite, to travel among the stars, through those groups illuminated by three or four suns orbiting under the influence of their mutual attraction. Ah! What a splendid sight! Stars shining in a thousand different shades. Days made of every color, of every hue of the rainbow, rising radiant on the horizon.

(*Murmurs of admiration.*)

Ox: That is our destination, gentlemen, and your Columbiad, which was used to fire a projectile to the Moon, will certainly be able to send that projectile over billions of leagues.

Barbicane: Yes! If you know the secret of making gunpowder that can generate a high enough velocity.

Ox: I have found a limitless expansive force, and soon, propelled by its all-powerful impetus, our projectile will have left the solar system behind.

Maston: Bravo, Dr. Ox! What a doctor, gentlemen, what a doctor!

Barbicane: And at what point in outer space will you aim the Columbiad?

Ox: At a new heavenly body, recently discovered by astronomers at the Cambridge Observatory,[10] the planet Altor.

All: Altor!

George: Yes! Altor! Altor!

Barbicane: All honor to the daring men who will undertake this conquest!

All: Hurrah! Hurrah!

Ox (*sarcastically*): Well, what do you say to that, Mr. Ardan?

Volsius: What do I say? I say nothing, Dr. Ox.

Ox: Not a word of blame or criticism of this daring undertaking by Hatteras?

Volsius: Why should I blame him, when it is my intention to go with him?

All: Ah!

Ox: What? You have the nerve . . . ?

Volsius: To be your companion, with your permission, Hatteras.

George: Oh, of course. You will go with us. You will share our glory.

Ox *(aside)*: We'll see about that.

Volsius: We'll meet in Florida, gentlemen, right beside the Columbiad.

Barbicane: We'll all be there.

All: Hurrah! Hurrah! Hurrah!

—SCENE 2—
THE CANNON SHOT

An open plain in Florida, in the southern United States. A gigantic cannon, of which only the lower part[11] is visible, is set up on its carriage at a slight angle from the vertical. In the background, an entire city with spires, houses, and trees. It is broad daylight.

(*Enter* Tartelet, Valdemar, *and* Maston.)

Maston: This is the place, gentlemen, to which I was to bring you.

Tartelet: Excuse me. To whom have we the honor of speaking?

Maston: Maston, a pure-blooded American.

Valdemar: Ah! Ah! Do you hear that, Tartelet? This gentleman is a purebred.

Maston: American. From generations back.

Valdemar: This gentleman comes from generations back.

Maston: American! Old stock.

Valdemar: This gentleman is an old stock.

Tartelet: Obviously.

Maston: Member of the Artillerymen's Club. I have invented a wonderful cannon.

Tartelet: Really?

Maston: A cannon with a range of 1250 feet . . . beyond the target.

Valdemar (*offering his hand*): What precision!

Tartelet: That's wonderful!

Maston: I have devised another whose projectile can knock down eight hundred men and two hundred horses at a single blow.

Tartelet: That's four men per horse.

Valdemar: Just like the Aymon brothers[12] in the time of Charlemagne.

Tartelet: But is it really infallible, sir?

Maston: I've been wanting to try it out. The horses said nothing, but the men stupidly refused to participate.

Tartelet: Well, I can understand that.

Valdemar: If you had used the other cannon, now, the one that carries 1,250 feet beyond the target, the horses would still have said nothing, but the men might have agreed more readily.

Tartelet: But why have you brought us here, sir?

Maston: Your colleague, Mr. George Hatteras, requests that you wait for him here, if you have definitely made up your minds to go with him on his next journey.

Tartelet: Our minds are made up, sir.

Valdemar: Of course, but where are we going?

Maston: To the land of the Altorians.

Valdemar: Altorians? Never heard of them.

Tartelet: What part of the world do they live in?

Maston: None.

Valdemar: What do you mean, none?

Maston: Exactly what I said. Altor is a recently discovered planet, and that's where you're going.

Valdemar: Just a minute! That's where we're going? And how, may I ask, are we going to get there?

Tartelet: Yes, how are we going to travel?

Maston *(turning and pointing to the huge cannon)*: There is your means of transportation.

Valdemar *(terrified)*: That? Come now, that's a. . . .

Tartelet: It's a cannon.

Valdemar: An immense cannon.

Maston: It's a Columbiad.

Valdemar and Tartelet: A Columbiad?

Maston: Equipped with a space capsule,[13] which, when propelled by several thousand kilos of picric acid,[14] will take you straight to the planet Altor.

Valdemar: And you think I'm going to get in there, with my seventeen-million-franc diamond? Oh no!

Maston: As you wish.

Valdemar: What about you, Tartelet? Are you going to be shot out of the cannon?

Tartelet *(calmly)*: Me? That depends.

Valdemar: Depends on what?

Tartelet *(to Maston)*: Will Miss Eva be going, too?

Maston: Definitely. She said nothing would keep her from her fiancé.

Tartelet: Well, nothing will keep me from her.

Valdemar: But that's madness, Tartelet!

Tartelet: You may be right, Valdemar, but when I came to the home of that young lady's grandmother, poor and hungry and friendless, those two wonderful women took me in, not as a beggar, but as a friend. That's why I followed Miss Eva when she left. And today, when a new and even greater danger stands in her way, should I abandon her, go quietly back to her grandmother, and say, "I deserted your granddaughter, madam. A man can't do as much out of gratitude as this child can do out of love"? No indeed! I would never dare to be so cowardly.

Valdemar (*touched*): Well, neither would I. And I won't leave you, Tartelet. What you have just said was very fine. You must come soon and live in my home. It will be a palace. My friendship, my table, my purse, and a little piece of my diamond will be yours, Tartelet.

(He kisses him on the cheek.)

Maston: You'll both go on the journey, then?

Valdemar (*energetically*): Yes, both of us. I wish we were already on the way. In fact, I wish we were already back again.

Tartelet: What time do we leave?

Maston: At twelve forty-two, by my chronometer.

Valdemar: Oh, by the way, before we leave I must go and see if my answer has arrived. They may have forgotten to bring it to me here.

Tartelet: What answer?

Valdemar: I sent another wire to that cruel Miss Babichok, telling her everything I've done and everything I'm still going to do, so she'll be sure to know. Ah! What a hero she'll have turned down, what a hero! Excuse me, gentlemen. *(Exit.)*

(Enter George *and* Ox, *from the right.)*

George: Here! Here it is!

Ox: This is the spot where you'll stand on the earth's surface for the last time.

Maston: And here is the gigantic cannon that will give you the first push toward the infinite.

Ox: Toward an older world than ours, whose inhabitants may already have invented everything that we have yet to invent.

George: So after going back into the past, to Atlantis, now we're going to head into the future.

Tartelet: But how are we going to get into that cannon?

Maston: You'll see. *(He touches a switch and the breech of the cannon opens, revealing the projectile, which also opens to show the interior fitted out like a cabin.)* You see, your space capsule is fitted out exactly like a first-class cabin.

George: So it is. But isn't it almost time to leave? Hurry! *(Aside to Ox)*: I don't want Eva to be exposed to any new dangers.

Ox *(in a low voice)*: Don't worry. She won't leave.

(Enter Volsius, Barbicane, *the members of the Gun Club, and a crowd of spectators.)*

Barbicane: We've come to say our last farewell, gentlemen. Is everything ready, Maston?

Maston: Everything.

(Enter an employee of the telegraph company.)

Tartelet: Ah! The man from the telegraph company! *(To the employee)*: You're looking for Mr. Valdemar, no doubt.

The Employee: Yes, sir.

Tartelet: You have a wire for him? Give it to me. I'll see that he gets it. *(He takes it and puts it in his pocket.)*

Maston: Twelve thirty-nine!

George: Let's go!

Ox: Yes! Let's go! Let's go!

Barbicane: Good-bye, then, my friends, good-bye. We'll cheer you on your way.

All: Hurrah! Hurrah! *(Cheers on all sides.)*

George: On to the infinite! On to the infinite!

    (Enter Valdemar, *running.)*

Valdemar: Ouf! I got here in time, I think.

Tartelet: Hurry up, Valdemar. We were going to leave without you.

Valdemar: Without me!

Tartelet: Will the gentlemen traveling to Altor please board the cannon.

Valdemar: The cannon!

Tartelet: Oh my goodness! What about Miss Eva?

Valdemar: And Mr. Ardan?

    (Enter Volsius *and* Eva.)

Volsius: Here we are, gentlemen. This young lady has asked me to accompany her.

George: Eva!

Ox: Silence! They are not going to leave.

Maston: At twelve forty-two I'll give the signal.

    (George and Ox *enter the capsule, followed by* Tartelet *and* Valdemar.)

Volsius: Come, Eva.

Eva: Yes! Yes! Come!

(They both head toward the cannon, but just as they are about to board it, the breech closes from the inside.)

Eva: Good God!

Volsius: Ah, doctor, you want to leave without us, do you? *(To Eva)*: Don't worry, my child. We'll get to the planet Altor before they do.

Maston's voice *(from below)*: Twelve forty-two. Fire!

(A detonation is heard, and the powerful recoil causes the Columbiad to sink far enough to reveal the landscape in the background. The spectators crowd around the cannon, waving their handkerchiefs and making the air resound with their cries.)

All: Hurrah! Hurrah!

— SCENE 3 —

THE PLANET ALTOR

A site on the planet Altor. In the distance, the outline of a city, apparently built of gold and silver. In the right foreground is the façade of a house whose walls are incrusted with precious stones.

(Enter several Altorians.)

First Altorian: As I said, this huge meteorite fell just a moment ago.

Second Altorian: I watched it fall, and as it came through the layers of air it made a frightful whistling sound.

First Altorian: It has to be taken to the museum. They've never had anything like it.

All: Yes! Yes!

First Altorian: Look! Look! The aerolite is opening.

Second Altorian: Two men are getting out.

First Altorian: Three . . . four men.

(Valdemar *and* Tartelet *emerge from the spaceship.*)

Valdemar (*lifting his feet very high as he walks*)**:** Why am I walking in this peculiar way?

Tartelet (*walking in the same way*)**:** I'm doing the same. What a peculiar way to walk!

Valdemar: My feet won't stay on the ground.

Tartelet: Neither will mine.

Valdemar (*to the inhabitants*)**:** Gentlemen, we are honored. Where is the planet Altor, please?

First Altorian: It's right here.

Valdemar: Well, I'm certainly glad to be here. (*Calling*) Hey! You over there! My worthy colleagues!

Tartelet: They'll come. They're exploring this unusual country.

Valdemar: Ah! We're on the planet Altor, then?

First Altorian: Yes. And you are from . . . ?

Tartelet: From planet Earth.

All the Altorians: From Earth?

Valdemar: But what's the city we see over there? (*He moves upstage.*)

First Altorian: It's our capital.

Tartelet: It looks as if it was built entirely of gold.

Valdemar: Wow! That would be worth going to see.

Tartelet: And will you be so kind as to take us there?

First Altorian: What do you mean? We will ask your permission to introduce you to our Academy of Sciences.

Tartelet: The Academy of Sciences?

First Altorian: And then you will be placed in the Museum of Natural History.

Valdemar: You mean . . . mounted?

Second Altorian: Oh no. Embalmed.

Tartelet: Embalmed? Just a minute, now.

First Altorian: Oh, later, only after you are dead.

Valdemar: That's very kind of you, sir.

Tartelet: Lead on, then. We'll follow you.

Valdemar: My goodness, it's a long way to the city! Couldn't we rest a little before we go on?

First Altorian: This is the home of a scientist who recently arrived with his daughter from the remotest regions of Altor. *(Pointing to a house on the right.)* He'll welcome you to his cottage.

Tartelet: A cottage! That? Its walls are studded with precious stones!

Valdemar: And the roof is thatched with gold! We're just beggars here. My diamond is worthless now. Here it is.

(He takes it out of his pocket.)

First Altorian: You'll find bigger and more beautiful diamonds than that lying on the ground wherever you go.

Valdemar: Damn!

First Altorian *(examining it)*: We don't even use them to pave our roads.

Valdemar: It isn't worth as much as an ordinary paving stone. I'm ruined! And I'm not going to keep it. Definitely not! *(Throwing it away)* Ah! Definitely not.

Tartelet: Well, I'd like to keep it as a souvenir of the center of our globe. *(He picks it up.)*

(Enter Volsius at the door of the cottage, dressed as an Altorian.)

Volsius: Foreigners?

Tartelet: Inhabitants of planet Earth, sir.

Volsius: Earth! A planet of the twenty-fifth magnitude, lighted by only a single sun.

Valdemar: Does he think that isn't enough?

Tartelet: Excuse me, sir. Do you have several suns here?

Volsius: Here there are two, and six moons that rise, one after the other, above the horizon of Altor.

Tartelet: Two suns?

Valdemar: Six moons! So if one of them deluneates—I mean, disappears from view. . . .

Tartelet: You still have five. You seem to be well informed about the planet we've just left.

Volsius: Yes, we know all about it. Two hundred thousand years of progress, from one generation to another, have brought us to the highest peak in every field. Our telescopes, whose magnification can be said to be unlimited, enable us to see your Earth as if it were less than a league away.

Tartelet: Splendid!

Volsius: But there are a few points on which our scientists would like some clarification. There is some kind of city with a small hill overlooking it, a river meandering through it, large buildings, squares, and people everywhere, many people, bustling about in the fog during the winter and in the dust during the summer. What is it?

Tartelet *(aside)*: A city that never gets watered. It must be Paris.

Volsius: We have distinctly made out a large public square with a bridge at one end. Across from the bridge there is a sort of palace in which a crowd of busy people gather. They obviously talk a lot and they never agree.

Valdemar: I know that country. I've been there. The bridge is called the Pont de la Concorde[15] and the palace at the end of it is called the Palace of Discor. . . . I mean, the Chamber of Deputies.[16]

Tartelet: Yes, it's the palace of the legislative body. *(Aside)* What was I going to do there?

Volsius: What goes on in this palace?

Valdemar: What goes on? Cabinet ministers get voted out of office.

Volsius: It also seems that in this city people jostle each other around from time to time. They fight, then they kiss, then they fight some more, then they kiss again.

Tartelet: That settles it! It's Paris, the capital of our fair land of France.

Valdemar: Paris. They eat beef, etc.

Volsius: Your country is not easy to govern, then.

Tartelet: And what about yours, sir?

Volsius: Ours? Well, that's different. It governs itself.

Tartelet: Governs itself?

Volsius: Yes, for several thousand years now we've been trying out every system of government: absolute government, which was overthrown by a constitutional monarchy, then constitutional government, which was overthrown by the Republic.[17]

Tartelet: And the Republic itself?

Volsius: Overthrown by the republicans.

Tartelet: And have you finally settled on something?

Volsius: Yes, we have no government at all.

Valdemar: And does it work?

Volsius: It works perfectly. In fact, it works too well, because the result of progress is that everyone has become scholarly. The shoemakers write poetry and the bakers take up astronomy. We haven't enough workers, and we'll get to the point where we have to pass a decree making ignorance compulsory.

Tartelet: You'll make ignorance compulsory?

Volsius: Another problem is a surplus population, which is becoming very awkward, since it increases every day, and the average life-span here is two or three hundred years.

Valdemar: People live for three hundred years here?

Volsius: Yes, sir.

Valdemar: Don't you have any doctors?

Volsius: We were foolish enough to abolish them. Since then, we've tried to train some new ones, but they haven't had time to make a thorough study of medicine, and the result is that they cure their patients.

Valdemar: Excuse me, but could you explain one small point for me, please? Why is it that here I feel as light as a feather? I'm walking around like a butterfly.

Tartelet: So am I. Without even trying, I lift my feet so high that it seems to me I must look like a rooster.

Valdemar: Or a turkey!

(They lift their legs very high as they walk.)

Volsius: It's very simple, gentlemen. Do you expend the same energy to walk on this planet as you did on your own?

Tartelet and Valdemar: Yes, of course.

Volsius: And since the mass of Altor is one-twentieth that of Earth, the gravitational pull toward the center is much weaker here, and your muscular strength appears to increase a hundredfold.

Tartelet: Ah, yes. I see.

Valdemar: I don't follow that at all.

Tartelet: So if I were to give dancing lessons here. . . .

Volsius: You would see your pupils leaping to unusual heights.

Tartelet: What if I were to do an entrechat?

Volsius (*laughing*)**:** You might fly away.

Valdemar: Don't do anything foolish, Tartelet. Don't try an entrechat.

Volsius: But I was told that four foreigners had arrived.

Tartelet: Our travelling companions aren't far away. They're busy studying the great construction works being carried out here.

(*Enter* George *and* Ox.)

Volsius: It's a gigantic project that our engineers have undertaken.

George: Yes, yes, it certainly is gigantic. Enormous gates and huge locks that seem designed to open a passage and let all the water in the ocean drain out of the bed that nature created for it.

Volsius: You're quite right. That is exactly what it is all about, gentlemen.

George: But why? What's the purpose?

Ox: This world on which we have just landed has been in existence for millions of years. It has exhausted the soil needed to feed its huge and growing population. It has exhausted the quarries needed to house them. It has dug bottomless mines to satisfy the needs of an extravagant civilization and industry, with the result that this planet is pitted everywhere with enormous holes, down to its uttermost depths.[18]

Valdemar: You mean we aren't safe here?

Volsius: No! Because the walls surrounding the central fire are no longer solid enough, and it threatens to break through to the outside.

Ox: And thousands of craters might open up at any minute.

Tartelet: Well! We chose a fine time to arrive!

Valdemar *(to* Volsius*):* Excuse me, sir. How do you get to Copenhagen from here?

Volsius: Don't worry. Our scientists tell us they have discovered a way to save us all from starving to death or being consumed by fire.

George: And how will they do that?

Ox *(sarcastically):* The first step is to cultivate the vast sea-covered plains by diverting the ocean through the huge cavities that I just mentioned, down into the center of this planet.

Volsius: Where it will extinguish the fire that threatens to break out.

George: Would they dare to carry out that momentous project?

Ox: That incredible madness!

George: It's a marvellous plan. I wish I could help to carry it out.

Volsius: Nothing could be easier. This is the day when the huge locks you saw just now will be opened. Come, gentlemen. Before we take you to our capital, my daughter and I will do the honors and show you around our house.

(George and Ox *head for the cottage on the right, followed by* Volsius.*)*

Tartelet *(takes out his handkerchief, and a piece of paper falls to the ground):* Well, well, what's that? Ah! It's the telegram for Valdemar that was handed to me back on Earth, and I forgot to give it to him. Hey! Valdemar! Valdemar!

(George, Ox, and Volsius *enter the cottage. As* Valdemar *is about to follow them,* Tartelet *takes him by the arm.)*

Valdemar: Mr. Tartelet!

Tartelet: My friend, just as we were about to take our places in the Columbiad, a telegram arrived for you.

Valdemar: A telegram? Where is it?

Tartelet: You weren't there yet. They handed it to me and—my goodness!—I must confess that I put it in my pocket and forgot about it.

Valdemar: Good God! It was an answer! An answer from Miss Babichok! Well, give it to me, then. Give it here!

Tartelet (*gives him the telegram*): Here it is.

Valdemar (*reads*): "Terrible event. At wedding banquet Cousin Finderup choked on fish bone." (*Sadly*) Dead! He's dead. Poor Finderup is d.... (*Smiling*) During the wedding banquet! Between noon and one o'clock. And Babichok is a widow! (*Cheerfully*) Ah! A widow, she's a widow, my friend. And on her wedding-day. Yes! Between noon and one o'clock. Ah!

Tartelet: Read the rest.

Valdemar: Yes, yes. I'll read it. (*Very sadly*) Cousin Finderup swallowed a fishbone. Cousin Finderup choked to death. (*Cheerily*) "Come back quickly. (*With feeling*) No matter if you are still a little overweight, if diamond is a lot overweight." (*Speaking*) Ah! That's so nice, so sweet, so tender!

Tartelet: Very tender. Yes.

Valdemar: Babichok, dear Babichok. She wants me. She's waiting for me. Quick, quick! I'll run to her. Horses! A carriage! A railway!

Tartelet: You want to travel through the limitless reaches of outer space in a carriage or a railway?

Valdemar: That's true. I wasn't thinking. So this is where you hand me that telegram!

Tartelet: Unfortunately, yes.

Valdemar: And when it arrived, I was only fifteen hundred leagues from Babichok.

Tartelet: So? It was just a little oversight.

Valdemar: Just a little oversight, he says! When Babichok is waiting for me, when she's free, a widow, choked to death—I mean, he is, Finderup. Are you aware, sir, that I'm entitled to hold you responsible for anything that may happen?

Tartelet: Responsible? Me? Really!

Valdemar (*angrily*): If she marries someone else, will you undertake to strangle that person, sir?

Tartelet: Mr. Valdemar, I advise you to use a more appropriate tone of voice when you speak to me, or else. . . .

Valdemar: Or else? Or else what? What?

Tartelet: Be careful, Mr. Valdemar.

Valdemar: Be careful yourself. And don't forget that on this planet my strength is ten times greater.

Tartelet: And so is mine, I suppose. And to prove it. . . . *(Bam!)* There!

(He gives him a vigorous kick in the seat of the pants. Valdemar goes flying two meters off the ground.)

Valdemar: Hey! What was that for?

(He falls to the ground.)

Tartelet (*laughs*): Ha, ha, ha! A weaker force of gravity. Point your toes out, sir, point your toes out!

Valdemar: Ah! You scoundrel!

(He kicks Tartelet.)

Tartelet (*flying into the air*): Ah!

(He falls back to the ground.)

Valdemar: A weaker force of gravity, sir. A weaker force of gravity. Sh! Someone's coming!

(Eva comes out of the building, dressed as a young Altorian woman.)

Eva: The door of my father's house is open to you, gentlemen.

Tartelet: Your. . . . Ah, yes. Excuse me, miss.

Eva: Your friends are waiting for you.

Valdemar: We'll join them now.

Tartelet *(threateningly)*: Whenever you wish, sir!

(They meet at the door.)

Valdemar *(in a friendly tone)*: After you.

Tartelet *(in the same tone)*: Go ahead.

Valdemar *(in the same tone)*: I couldn't possibly.

Tartelet: Well, then, if you insist.

(They both go in at the same time.)

Eva *(dreamily)*: My mysterious protector has told me that George will soon recover his sanity, but perhaps for the last time. And this must be the place where our cruel enemy will put him through a trial that would destroy him. Oh, I don't want to be a stranger in his eyes any longer. My reason for following him was to share his danger. I'll make myself known to him, but only to him. Dr. Ox still keeps looking at me, but he hasn't recognized me.

(Enter Ox.)

Ox: There she is! It's really her.

Eva: It's him!

Ox: Just a moment, please.

Eva: My father is waiting for me. If you will excuse me. . . .

Ox: The man who is in there is not your father, and I recognize you.

Eva: Well, I don't know you.

Ox: I don't know what power or what miracle has brought you here, but you are Eva, and you know that I. . . .

Eva: I don't know you, I said.

Ox: All right then, I was mistaken. To tell the truth, I'm not sorry. It would have been painful for me to let the young lady of whom I spoke witness what is going to happen here.

Eva: What is going to happen?

Ox: It would have been painful for me, I say, to have her present, not at her fiancé's madness, but at his death.

Eva *(forgetting herself)*: He's going to die! George!

Ox *(forcefully)*: As you see, I was not mistaken.

Eva: Well, yes. I gave myself away. Yes, I'm Eva, but what do you expect now that you have forced this confession from me? What do you want from me?

Ox: I want to try one last time to convince you, and to soften your heart.

Eva: And what about your heart? Has it softened? Have you finished persecuting me, then?

Ox: This is not you, it's him! The rival I hate!

Eva: But he is my whole life.

Ox: Don't say that!

Eva: He is my very soul.

Ox: Hush!

Eva: He is all my happiness, all my love.

Ox *(forcefully)*: Enough! Enough, I tell you.

Eva: And you think you can win me by murdering him! You kill me, and you want me to love you! Well, let me tell you this: I feel as much hostility toward you as you feel toward George, whom I love. You hate him. I hate you.

Ox *(beside himself)*: Eva! But what is happening to me? The anger and hatred in your voice have penetrated to the very depths of my soul. Ah! Perhaps I could resign myself to the pain of not being loved by you. But to be hated? Never! Have I uncovered the most fearsome secrets of nature, and acquired superhuman knowledge, only to have it all crumble miserably at the feet of a child? Ah! It's just as Captain Nemo said: it's in your own heart that she will find weapons to use against you. Ah, yes! My pride is vanquished, yes, my heart is broken. I beg you, I entreat you, I fall at your feet. Don't hate me, Eva. Don't hate me.

(He drags himself after her and tries to take her hand.)

Eva *(pulling her hand away)*: Leave me alone. Leave me alone!

Ox: Have pity on me, Eva. Listen. Do you want me to be your humble servant, your slave?

Eva: No!

Ox: Well then, here. A thousand times more. I'll be his slave. . . . George's. Ah, that would be a very great sacrifice, and very painful, I can tell you. Never mind. Just say a word of compassion, of pity, and I'll do it. Only don't hate me. Don't hate me. Eva, don't hate me!

(Enter Volsius.)

Volsius: My daughter!

(Eva slowly enters the house. Ox makes as if to follow her. Volsius bars his way, and they stare at each other, face to face.)

Ox: Eva!

Volsius: "The woman shall crush thy head under her heel."

Ox *(still watching Eva)*: Has this terrible curse come down through the centuries to fall on me? No, I'll triumph over this love. I'll tear it out of my heart. Ah, but I can't! I'll never be able to! "The woman will crush thee under her heel."

(The scene changes.)

— SCENE 4 —

THE END OF A WORLD

An immense square surrounded by palaces of a special architecture. The walls are built of precious stones and the most beautiful marble. Gold and silver are everywhere. There is a dazzling light, which has all the intensity of electric lights.

(*A magnificent celebration is under way. Full goblets are passed among the groups.*)

(*Enter* George, Eva, Ox, Tartelet, Valdemar, *Altorian men and women.*)

(*BALLET*)

(*A ballet performed by Altorian women is abruptly interrupted at its height by a great sound of bells and drums.* George *rushes in among the dancers, followed by the others.*)

George: The hour has struck, and the gigantic project is being accomplished at this very moment. Through these colossal gates, which I opened with my own hands, I saw the sea pour into the abyss with a roar. I saw it fall in enormous cataracts, and the resounding noise of its fall was answered by the prolonged rumbling of subterranean fires. It seemed as if that whole mass of fire was in revolt against an enemy invasion, and great clouds of purple smoke rose up from the struggle of those two furious elements. Sing! Drink! Dance! You have achieved an unparalleled accomplishment, a glorious triumph of man over nature, a magnificent spectacle, which anyone would give his life to see.

(*Enter* Volsius.)

Volsius: And soon you will all pay for it—with your lives,

All: Ah!

Eva: What did he say?

Ox *(sarcastically, in a powerful voice)*: He said, poor fools that you are, that a terrible cataclysm is about to occur, which you yourselves have brought about. The water that you have sent rushing into the planet's central furnace will not extinguish it, but will be transformed into thick vapors, which will overturn and destroy everything, and the wreckage of this planet will be scattered through outer space.

George *(delirious)*: Well, they'll take us with them to other solar systems.

Volsius: I tell you, Altor has only a few more minutes to live.

George *(picking up a goblet)*: Let's drink, my friends, let's drink. If death is to strike us down, let's die with a final song of triumph on our lips.

Eva: Let's die with a final prayer.

Half of the people: Yes, yes! Let's drink! Let's drink!

The other half *(bowing)*: Let's pray.

(Those on one side begin to dance, while those on the other side pray.)

— S C E N E   5 —

T H E   E X P L O S I O N

Suddenly, there is a frightful explosion. Everything collapses at once in smoke and flames and is swallowed up. Nothing is left but a few shapeless ruins. The sky is covered with clouds crisscrossed by flashes of lightning. Thunder rumbles. All the characters are knocked down and appear to be dead. Only Ox and Volsius remain standing. They look at each other defiantly. A curtain of smoke rises slowly toward the friezes and gradually hides the ruins and the people.

— S C E N E   6 —

A N D E R N A K   C A S T L E

The salon of Andernak Castle as it appeared in the first scene of Act I. George *is lying on a sofa, with* Eva *kneeling beside him.* Mme de Traventhal *is beside* Eva. Tartelet *is standing a little to one side.* Volsius *and* Dr. Ox *are at the patient's bedside.*

Mme de Traventhal: The poor lad. This is not the condition I had hoped to find him in when he came back.

Eva: Oh God! Will he live? And if he does, will he ever recover his sanity?

Tartelet *(aside)*: Alas! I'm very much afraid he may not.

Volsius: Don't give up hope, my child. Dr. Ox and I, between us,[19] may bring about a double miracle.

Ox: Between us? What do you mean by that?

Volsius: You are a powerful incarnation of that science for which the body is everything, and which believes in no future life. I, on the other hand, am a humble believer, and I consider our earthly environment as nothing. Restore life to this body. Say to it, "Rise up and walk!" I will do all in my power to rekindle his reason and restore calm and strength to his immortal soul.

Ox: You want me to save him? Me?

Eva: "I will be your slave and his, if I am no longer hated," you told me. I renounce all hatred. Save him.

(He pours a few drops of a potion from a vial onto George's *lips.)*

Ox: And now, wait!

Tartelet: Let's wait. *(He sees* Valdemar *enter.)* Valdemar, sh!

(He signals to him not to make any noise.)

Valdemar *(in a low voice, drawing* Tartelet *to one side)*: Yes, Tartelet, it's me. I'm very happy but also very upset.

Tartelet: What's the matter, then?

Valdemar: I saw Babichok again. She was waiting for me, but she was also waiting for my diamond, and you know, back there, on the planet, where it was worthless, I foolishly threw it away.

(He bursts into tears.)

Tartelet: Yes, and I picked it up. I did!

Valdemar *(sadly)*: Ah, you picked it up, Tartelet?

Tartelet: And I'm going to give it back to you, Valdemar.

Valdemar: You're giving it back to me? Tartelet, my friend! We'll present it to Babichok, both of us, and we'll marry her, both of. . . . No!

Ox: Look, his eyes are about to open. His mouth is about to speak. He's raising himself up.

George: Ah!

Ox: He's speaking.

George (*completely delirious*)**:** Where are we? Ah! The center of the earth. Eva is going to die. She is saved! Now. . . . The sea. . . . Atlantis, my kingdom, and my triumph.

Eva: Alas! He's still in the grip of madness.

Volsius: Now it's my turn.

(*He goes over to the organ and begins to play.*)

George: Altor! The planet Altor! A whole world annihilated. Some were singing and drinking. Others were praying. (*During this last speech, the scene has changed and represents a sort of aerial cathedral.*) They're praying. And here is the heavenly sanctuary. I hear angel voices. Ah, I feel a healing calm spreading throughout my entire being. My forehead is cooler and the veil that obscured my thoughts is lifting. Yes, yes! I remember. I see. I recognize you, all of you. (*Taking* Eva's *hand.*) Eva! Ah, dear Eva! I love you. No more mad dreams. I'm yours and yours alone—forever.

Valdemar: I'm yours, Babichok. Your Valdemar.

Tartelet (*giving him the diamond*)**:** Your Valdemar and his diamond!

(Valdemar *throws himself into* Tartelet's *arms.*)

⌐SCENE 7⌐

ÆPOTHEOSIS

Volsius *now plays a kind of Hosanna. The cathedral is transformed again. A shining Gloria appears at the back, surrounded by angels. Even Ox, over-come by the sublimity of this vision, bows his head.*

THE END

1882

TWO REVIEWS OF JOURNEY THROUGH THE IMPOSSIBLE

he first review was written by a professional Parisian reviewer, Arnold Mortier, who, year after year, set down his impressions and feelings in books entitled *Les soirées parisiennes 18xx* (*The Parisian Evenings of 18xx*) and signed "A Gentleman Sitting in the Orchestra" ("Un monsieur de l'orchestre"). These books were published every year by the Parisian publisher Dentu. Mortier wrote his review just after the opening night performance, November 25, 1882. This review was written in French and was translated by Edward Baxter.

The second review was published in the *New York Times*, December 19, 1882 (page 2, column 1). The author, who is unknown, was probably the Paris correspondent for the *Times*. This review was written in English on December 4, 1882.

Arnold Mortier

EVENINGS IN PARIS
IN 1882

JOURNEY THROUGH
THE IMPOSSIBLE

NOVEMBER 25

There is no need for me to discuss the merits of the fantasy play that has just opened at the Porte-Saint-Martin Theatre.[1] D'Ennery[2] and Jules Verne already have *Around the World in Eighty Days* and *Michel Strogoff* to their credit. They have made money for two production teams, their two stage plays have been performed a thousand times, and it is not hard to understand why M. Paul Clèves[3] should have begged the two eminent collaborators to let him have their *Journey Through the Impossible*, even though the script of this play had been abandoned by its authors several times, taken up again, then abandoned once more. It must have been tempting to use M. Verne's most popular novels and the most important of his extraordinary and curious short stories, which have brought pleasure to children the world over, to borrow an episode here and a character there and turn it all into a kind of serious fairy tale in which rondeaus and couplets would be replaced by soliloquies and lectures, but d'Ennery, with that profound knowledge of the theater that is one of his greatest strengths, had acknowledged at first that it could not be done. What made him change his mind, I cannot say. The fact remains that last spring he finally promised to give M. Clèves the long-desired play.

I must point out first of all that the manager of the Porte-Saint-Martin staged a very lavish production of the play, that he provided d'Ennery and Verne with everything they needed to make it a success, and that, all in all, the production is very beautiful and very elegant.

My one criticism of the production is that it lacks imagination, novelty, and ingenuity. The sets are lovely, but we are familiar with them all because we have seen them countless times in countless stage plays. The costumes are dazzling, often graceful, but they lack originality. The ballets are brilliant, danced by pretty girls as scantily clad as possible. They must have cost M. Clèves a pretty penny. He has never done anything better and never spent more, but the little poetic note, so essential to ballets, even in fairy tales, is totally absent. In short, a great deal of money went into this production, but very few ideas.

ACT I: THE EARTH

Act I opens as a private drama, in the immense hall of a castle, with high vaulted ceilings. It must surely not be easy to heat that room. Note that we are in Denmark.

Following the announcement, "Doctor Ox!" a low whispering is heard among the spectators, who have possibly not forgotten Dupuis in the operetta by Offenbach.

It is not Dupuis who comes on stage, however, but Taillade,[4] as Doctor Miracle, dressed all in black, sombre and diabolical, as befits a character who is to portray the Evil Genie for an entire evening.

To oppose him, Joumard, looking the perfect clergyman, is the incarnation of the Good Genie.

In the cheery old fairy tales of our fathers' time, these two genies were invariably portrayed by two little women with no talent whatsoever, pleasant-looking creatures who kept the show moving along by holding out their magic wands. Mlle Mariani, Mlle Delval, and many others became specialists in this genre. Is it not time, perhaps, to return to that practice?

There is an organ in the play at the Porte-Saint-Martin, as there is in the one at the Ambigu.[5] This is a luxury that the popular theaters have not often indulged in. While Joumard pretends to be eliciting dulcet tones from the instrument, a celestial apparition lights up the backstage area. It is the archangel Michael overthrowing the Devil. The effect is somewhat poetic, except that the wires supporting the good and evil angels seem to me to be too heavy. It destroys the illusion, but it is more prudent, and besides, it puts the lie to the proverb "No one is obliged to do the impossible."

At the end of the first scene, all the characters drink a potion, which instantly transports them to Naples.

This is referred to in the hall as the "express-train beverage." Is there a sleeping-car in the bottle?

No sooner are we in Naples than the journey begins. The heroes descend to the center of the earth through the crater of Vesuvius. And Dailly[6] is a member of the exploration party—thank God!

My goodness, if I am ever in grave danger, if I am about to be shipwrecked at sea, in a carriage drawn by a terrified horse, or in a balloon with the gas escaping through a fatal tear, I hope—and this is a very selfish wish on my part—I hope Dailly will be nearby. I will look at his round, honest, constantly beaming face, his cheerful mouth, to which fear is powerless to bring a scowl, and come what may, I will laugh. I will keep laughing, and if I sink beneath the waves, if I crash onto the cobblestones, I will go down laughing. Anything can be endured, if Dailly is there.

The descent to the center of the earth occurs in a very uncomplicated manner. For a moment Taillade and young Volny can be seen painfully making their way along a rock that looks like a bridge across the abyss. Then the sets begin to rise, not only the backstage tapes-tries, but the framework and all the scenery. This rise, which simulates a descent, is extremely well contrived, and is a fine tribute to M. Courbois, the Porte-Saint-Martin's highly skilled set designer.

We travel through diamond country, where—wonder of wonders, and very difficult to explain in a play that claims to be scientific!—the diamonds are found already cut. I would encourage the set designer, M. Poisson, to examine the tremendous difference between a cut diamond and a rough one. Then we reach the region of stalactites, reminiscent of the interior of the cave in Monceau Park,[7] but on a larger scale.

Enter the degenerate creatures, the inhabitants of the center of the earth. They are clothed in ash-colored rags, their long hair is dirty gray, and their faces are green and deathly pale. These citizens of the earth's entrails appear to be very ill indeed.

"Their bowels must ache from living in the bowels of the earth," said someone sitting close to me.

Joumard takes up his violin and plays them a tune by M. Lagoanère,[8] and the degenerate creatures, charmed and ecstatic, withdraw, seeming to murmur "encore."

At last we come to the region of fire, the eternal red backdrop, with copper lamé, gold sequins, and strips of golden gauze.

Now comes the ballet of the Salamanders, which I personally did not much care for, but which produced a tremendous effect. It is a hodge-podge of leotards representing silver coats of mail, with steel fittings and steel sequins, costumes of fiery red and golden yellow, dia-monds, pearls, a whole host of shining, glittering, shimmering, flashing things, a quantity of costly accessories, all lit up by a garish light, to which is added, toward the end, the red glow of Bengal lights. It is the ultimate in gaudiness.

There is nothing artistic whatsoever about the end of this act, but it was a hit this evening and will probably be a hit in the days to come—which, for M. Clèves, is all that matters.

ACT II: THE SEA

All the sets for the second act are the work of M. Rubé[9] and M. Chaperon,[10] and I can assure you that they are recognizable as such. From a decorative point of view, this second act is absolutely remarkable, and I deeply regret the cuts that it was considered necessary to make since yesterday's dress rehearsal. It is impossible to imagine, for example, anything prettier, warmer, or better depicted than the harbor of Goa where the action of the first scene takes place.

In this scene, Dailly, haggling with the Indian over the price of his diamond, was supposed to say to him, "My friend, you are a goa-illeur"![11]

But he decided against it. That would come later.

An admirably painted backdrop depicts the open sea, with the *Nautilus* plowing the waves like a gigantic whale. M. Lagoanère's music imitates the roaring of the waves. Then, in a very short scene, we see Taillade standing on the *Nautilus*, which now creates the illusion of a rock in mid-ocean. Taillade has obviously thought very carefully about the impression he will make. To see him here, one might think he was Chateaubriand[12] at Saint-Malo.[13]

Now we are inside the *Nautilus*, with Joumard disguised as Captain Nemo. This excellent actor had put on the expressive and friendly face of Jules Verne, but since the audience might have thought the author of the *Voyages extraordinaires* was coming on stage to stop the performance, Joumard was requested to abandon that tack.

The scene changes. Yesterday, at the dress rehearsal, we were at the bottom of the sea. It was a second edition of the aquarium from *Peau d'âne*, marvellously reworked by Rubé and Chaperon. The coral reefs formed huge rocks on which grew anemones (those living flowers), madrepores, the whole gamut of underwater vegetation, so beautiful, so colorful, and so interesting that one never grows tired of admiring it. Fish were playing about in the clear water. Sturgeons swam quickly by, gilt-heads dived and came back up, fat gurnards wriggled along, followed by enormous crabs and octopuses with phosphorescent eyes.

One octopus was almost a personal enemy to Dailly. At one point it wrapped its tentacles around him and raised him to a considerable height, hanging upside down. Needless to say, the effect on this excellent actor's digestion was somewhat negative, to say nothing of the fact that the tentacles were scraping the skin off his fingers.

"I never did like octopus," said Dailly, "and today I despise it."

Fortunately for him, the octopus was no longer on stage when the act came to an abrupt end with the resurrection of the city of Atlantis—still at the bottom of the sea. The set designers and costume designers, having no documents to guide them, decided to create a scene that is a mixture of Egyptian, Indian, Syrian, Roman, Greek, and Arabic. But it is beautifully colored and very luxurious. There are many magnificent processions, and great quantities of jewels, expensive props, golden helmets, silver shields, banners, palm leaves, fans. Note that there are a dozen horses on stage (sea horses, no doubt) and that their riders suddenly begin to play, for no particular reason, the war march from *Michel Strogoff*. The overall effect is pleasant, although we are not quite sure what we have just seen.

ACT III: THE SKY

The authors begin by ushering us into the Gun Club, that amusing and witty invention found in *From the Earth to the Moon*. M. Barbicane is in the chair and calls for silence by repeatedly firing his revolver.

Joumard appears in a new incarnation, this time as Michel Ardan, with the red moustache, jacket, and familiar gray hat of M. Nadar.[14]

The second scene of this act, painted by Poisson, is charming. It is a terrace from which one has a bird's eye view of the city and part of the Columbiad, the colossal cannon that will send some of the play's characters, not to the Moon, but much farther, to the planet Altor.

All roads to Altor are open!

The cannon goes off and our friends suddenly find themselves among the Altorians. You understand, of course, that the only reason for going so far is to watch a ballet, the ballet of the Altorians, the prettiest of the three.

The costumes for this ballet are a little short on fantasy, but they are adorable, charmingly made, exquisite in color, and very varied. There are bird-catchers with their caged birds of paradise; flower vendors bending under the weight of multicolored roses; newlywed couples with lively bouquets of orange blossoms; pearl divers (both men and women) carrying large golden nets and, on their backs, golden baskets full of fine stones; dancing girls clad in fish skin and others covered with pearls; and finally, the Altorian boaters, the men looking very naughty, with an ornament resembling a change purse strangely placed at one of the most conspicuous parts of their costume. The men and women in the boats conclude by forming an immense boat with banners, flag-covered masts, and golden oars. It is really very pretty.

But the planet's last day has sounded. Everything crumbles, everything vanishes, night falls, and we are back in the Danish castle where the play began.

The back of the theater opens once more and we see, like an apotheosis, an interior corner of Notre Dame,[15] then an immense cathedral that seems to rise to the very heavens.

There is a mystical note at the end. But M. Clèves's honor is saved. It can be said that, in order to make a success of this *Journey Through the Impossible*, he has attempted the impossible.

The New York Times

A JULES VERNE PIECE

PUBLISHED DECEMBER 19, 1882

Paris, Dec. 4.—Naturally the union of those two great minds, M. Jules Verne and M. A. Dennery, could not fail to produce a play that would be worth seeing. For months we have been promised marvels by M. Paul Clèves, and he has kept his promise in one sense by producing the piece entitled by the authors and the Porte St. Martin's manager "Un Voyage à Travers l'Impossible," a fantastical piece in three [acts] and 22 [scenes]. The three [acts] are: "The Earth," "The Sea," and "The Sky;" the 22 [scenes] represent episodes therein, and illustrate the ways and manners of the inhabitants of the center of the globe, of ocean's depths, and of the starry firmament. To show up these, M. Verne has selected the most striking incidents of his romantico-scientific productions, such as "Doctor Ox," *A Journey to the Moon*, and *A Journey to the Bottom of the Sea*, and M. Dennery has patched them together, the collaboration resulting in a salmagundi, pretty nearly headless and tailless, yet which must be acknowledged to be a triumph of stage carpentry, scene-painting, and costumery. This is the plot, if plot it can be called: in a little town of Denmark lives the Widow Traventhal, whose daughter is betrothed to young George Hatteras. George is a son of that famous Captain Hatteras whose voyage in search of the North Pole terminated fatally. His friends have always concealed the parentage: they feared lest the example of the father might tempt the child, but it is all in vain; no man can escape his destiny. The blood of the bold navigator courses through his veins; he thirsts after the unknown: he, lives in the midst of maps and charts and globes, and in his delirium dreams of explorations such as none other has ever imagined. He would attempt the impossible. "Quite mad!" say his fellow-citizens. "Certainly very sick!" reply Madame and Mademoiselle Traventhal, who forthwith send for Doctor Ox and ask him to prescribe. Now, Doctor Ox is an excellent scientist by repute, but Doctor Ox, instead of administering chloral or bromide of potassium, as assuredly would have done the eminent Dr. Charcot, the present authority in lunatic and nervous affections, works up the diseased brain of his patient, first, by revealing to him his connection with the deceased Arctic explorer; second, by the assurance that he can help him to realize his desire to become another Christopher Columbus. The doctor is a species of Mephistopheles; he, too, is in love with Heva[1]—I write her name with an H this time, but your readers may suit themselves as to the orthography, about which there has been as much controversy among newspaper reporters as there was over the letter *gamma* in Gounod's "Tribut de Zamora,"[2] where many contended that this consonant ought to be doubled. The savant's scheme is truly diabolical; he administers an elixir which emancipates the youth from subjection to physical laws that hamper ordinary human beings, but his real object is to get rid of his rival by death or incurable madness. In vain does the organist Volsius try to snatch George from the sinister influence; he tries music, he tries argument, and he might as well have left both untried, for George persists, and then, with a noble spirit of self-sacrifice, he assures the disconsolate maiden that he, too, will share the perils of her lover's peregrinations. He will protect him, he swears, in spite of himself, and this he does in a series of avatars wherein he appears as Professor Lidenbrock, Captain Nemo, Michel Ardan, and an Altorian—this, I should explain, means a citizen of the planet Altor—whither the travelers go in a bombshell fired from a monster Columbiad situated in the garden of the Gun Club of Baltimore. You must understand that the struggle between the doctor and the musician is intended to illustrate the conflict between good and evil. But Heva is not altogether satisfied; she fears to trust her George to Volsius alone, and so she, too, and with her a friend of the family, one Tartelet,[3] the dancing-master, takes a dose of the magic mixture, and in the twinkling of an eye Ox, George, Volsius, Heva, and the dancing-master are transported by an "electric current" to the foot of Mount Vesuvius, and then begins the dance.

The tourists, whose party is reinforced by a traveler from Sweden,[4] whom they meet at Naples, Monsieur Valdemar by name, begin their excursions by a visit to the "entrails of the earth" in search of the "central fire." Three "entrails" are visited in this journey, of which a fissure in the volcano was the starting point; the first entrail is a rocky cavern; the second struck me as made of granite; in the third is represented a most fantastic subterranean vegetation, with the atmosphere rendered peculiarly luminous, giving to an underground rivulet extraordinary effects of light and color. These regions are inhabited by the Troglodytes, a degenerate class of beings, ugly, but picturesque, with long hair, mud-tinted faces, and silver hands, who, much struck by Heva's beauty, rush savagely at the intruder, and are calmed as suddenly by Professor Lidenbrock, by whom is executed, quite sweetly, an air on his pocket violin. At the first performance M. Joumard did something from the "Tribut de Zamorra;" at the sixth he selected something from *Carmen*.[5]

This [setting] is numbered six on the programme. In [set] seven the central furnace has been reached. I suppose that this reality may be qualified as a fourth and final entrail, as, after 50 or 60 lovely beings, attired in very dark blue with gold trimmings, gold helmets, and black kid gloves reaching above the elbows, have danced and capered, another company of white ladies representing fountains, dance frantically, and the curtain falls, thus giving it to be understood that, Earth having no more mysteries to reveal to G. H., he and his friends may try another kingdom.

Setting eight is the roadstead of Goa, with Indian pavilions on the right and left, and in the background the city and the sea. Here, Monsieur Valdemar, the funny man, does a monologue expressive of his satisfaction with the "diamond picked up 5,000 feet below the surface of the earth;" then the Nautilus, a cigar-shaped craft, steams in: the travelers go on board, and in the eleventh [setting] are seen seated around the hospitable table of Captain Nemo—the third incarnation of Volsius. In the twelfth [setting] the Nautilus has plunged, and her passengers walk out of their cabins into the magic city of the Atlantides, which, you know, was swallowed up ever so long ago by the angry floods. The citizens of this realm have a revolution; they want a king, and, having chosen one of themselves, are about to crown him, when Mademoiselle Patry,[6] a very handsome person, combines with Doctor Ox and George to make a coup d'état, which results in the selection of the hero and his immediate coronation, all serving as a pretext for more dancing, more marble staircases, porphyry columns, minarets, and properties in general, outdoing, perhaps, in splendor the brilliant display in the "Mille et Une Nuits." [Setting fourteen], The Gun Club of Baltimore, offers nothing especially interesting or original. The members amuse themselves by shooting pistols while the big gun is being made ready. A servant enters, and the columbiad is prepared. "Gentlemen," he announces, "will the intending travelers kindly take seats in the shell!" With the exception of Doctor Ox, the party get into the projectile—in the slips, for we never see the monster projectile—and, the scene changing, the huge mortar, "warranted to carry with the utmost precision 1,250 feet beyond the point aimed at," appears pointed toward the firmament. Just as the match is being applied, Monsieur Volsius rushes on the stage and insists on an excursion ticket, which is kindly granted by the Gun Club of Baltimore's committee. He gets in at the vent: an explosion is heard, and again the scene shifts to the planet Altor. The car has reached [its] destination in safety; they are met by Maître Volsius as an Altorian in a long robe like a Jewish rabbi's crimson silk cap, a sort of caricature of Louis XI, to whom Messieurs Valdemar and Tartelet make a political speech in explanation of the advantages and disadvantages of parliamentarianism, while their companions admire the architectural beauties of a planet where a cottage has a golden roof and walls encrusted with precious stones. Another circumstance much impresses the party; the Altorians are favored with two suns—one for the day, the other for the night. Valdemar ingenuously remarks: "What a pity that there is not a third in case of an eclipse." This intensely witty joke is immensely applauded always. During their journey some of the travelers have changed their toilets. Heva looks very gorgeous in a gown with white satin, above which is a tunic of white merino, profusely embroidered and trimmed with green marabout feathers, and a corsage of currant-colored satin, with white jet and gauze sleeves.

It is on the marketplace of Altor that we are treated to the third and most magnificent ballet of the piece—palaces, terraces, colonnades, galleries; nothing is wanting to give effect to this spectacle, than which nothing more beautiful has been produced, even at the Académie Nationale de Musique. Suddenly, in the midst of mirth and joy, comes a terrible crash; a "meteoric comet" has struck the festive planet; everything crumbles away; the clouds gather, the thunder rolls, the lightning flashes, and Altor becomes a thing of the past. How the excursionists escape the cataclysm is not explained, but they do escape in some way or another; they get back to Earth, where, in the nineteenth [setting]—the "Castle of Andernach"—George, at first quite insane, recovers his reason, thanks to his betrothed, whose love triumphs over the jealous hate of the fatal doctor, after which comes the obligatory apotheosis in three transformations and the curtain falls definitively. And now, if you wish, an opinion of the merits of the "Journey Through the Impossible," I will say frankly that I have never seen anything more idiotically incoherent, or of which the dialogue is more pretentious. Under another name it is only a re-edition of "Pilules du Diable," the "Biche au Bois," the "Mille et Une Nuits," which again are only speaking versions of the old-fashioned pantomimes. George is Harlequin, Heva Columbine, Volsius the Good

Genius, Valdemar a good-natured Clown, and Doctor Ox the Wicked Enchanter. These adventures and mishaps have been seen a hundred times before, and if the people did not talk they would be all the better liked. Yet, for all that, the piece is successful—an immense success and a success which will last for months, as panoramas nowadays are all the fashion. M. Paul Clèves has given proof of taste and of unrivaled prodigality, and I should not be surprised if the "Voyage à Travers l'Impossible" equaled in vogue the famous "Tour du Monde." Still, I think that it will prove to be M. Verne's "Song of the Swan"; That this will be the last trial of scientifico-fantastico-geographical dramas.

Notes

ACKNOWLEDGMENTS

1. Edward Baxter's translations of Jules Verne are *Family without a Name* (Toronto: NC Press, 1982), *The Fur Country* (Toronto, NC Press, 1987), *[The] Invasion of the Sea* (Middletown, Conn.: Wesleyan University Press, 2001), *The Humbug—The American Way of Life* (in: *The Jules Verne Encyclopedia*, edited by Brian Taves and Stephen Michaluk Jr. [Lanham, Md.: Scarecrow Press, 1996], pp. 73–85).

INTRODUCTION

1. *Vingt mille lieues sous les mers* (Paris: Hetzel, 1869–1870).

2. *De la Terre à la lune* (Paris: Hetzel, 1865).

3. A complete bibliography of Verne's works (novels, short stories, plays, etc.) can be found at www.jv.gilead.org.il/biblio/.

4. The most important French publisher of the nineteenth century,

Pierre-Jules Hetzel (1814–1886) published Alphonse Daudet, Alexandre Dumas, Charles Dickens, Théophile Gautier, and Jules Verne. His illustrators were, among many others, Léon Benett, Emile Bayard, Georges Bertall, Gustave Doré, Eugène Froment, Tony Johannot, and Ernest Messonier. In 1873, he turned the management of the publishing company over to his son, Louis-Jules Hetzel, who eventually sold it to Hachette in 1914.

5. *Le Sphinx des glaces* (Paris: Hetzel, 1897).

6. *Astounding Stories* 16, no. 6 (February 1936): 8–32; 17, no. 1 (March 1936): 125–55; 17, no. 2 (April 1936): 132–50.

7. New York: Harper & Brothers, 1838.

8. *Voyages extraordinaires*. This title was given to the collection of Verne's novels by Hetzel after the publication of the first four novels. In the introduction to the first volume (*Hatteras*), Hetzel wrote, "The goal of the series is, in fact, to outline all the geographical, geological, physical, and astronomical knowledge amassed by modern science and to recount, in an entertaining and picturesque format that is his own, the history of the universe" (translated by Arthur B. Evans).

9. "Jules Verne at Home," *Temple Bar* no. 129 (June 1904): 664–71.

10. Adolphe Philippe (1811–1899), known as Adolphe d'Ennery, was a French playwright whose best-known piece, *Les Deux orphelines* (*The Two Orphans*), was performed on Broadway in 1874, 1904, and 1926. His wife's collection of oriental art (belonging to the State) can still be visited today in Paris (Musée d'Ennery).

11. *Cinq semaines en ballon* (Paris: Hetzel, 1863).

12. *Le Tour du monde en quatre-vingts jours* (Paris: Hetzel, 1873).

13. *Michel Strogoff* (Paris: Hetzel, 1876).

14. *Les Enfants du capitaine Grant* (Paris: Hetzel, 1867–1868).

15. *Les Voyages au théâtre* (Paris: Hetzel, 1881).

16. Barbara M. Barker, ed., *Bolossy Kiralfy: Creator of Great Musical Spectacles (An Autobiography)* (Ann Arbor & London: UMI Research Press, 1988).

17. Alexandre Dumas père (1802–1870), a French novelist and playwright of the romantic period. He is best remembered for his historical novels *The Three Musketeers* (*Les trois mousquetaires*, 1844) and *The Count of Monte-Cristo* (*Le Comte de Monte-Cristo*, 1844). He sponsored Jules Verne at the beginning of the young writer's literary career.

18. Theater built by Alexandre Dumas in 1846 and opened in 1847. His plays as well as those of Shakespeare, Goethe, Calderon, Schiller, and others, were performed until 1850 when the theater went bankrupt.

19. *Les Pailles rompues* (Paris: Beck, 1850). Performed June 12, 1850.

20. One of the main private theaters in Paris, besides the Comédie française and the Opéra, both of which belonged to the government.

21. Hector Berlioz (1803–1869), French composer and creator of the *Symphonie fantastique* (1831).

22. Charles-François Gounod (1818–1893), French composer and creator of *Faust* (1859).

23. Georges Bizet (1838–1875), French composer and creator of *Carmen* (1875).

24. Adolphe-Charles Adam (1803–1867), French composer and creator of *Si j'étais roi* (1852).

25. Witty and cynical lyrical composition (created by Jacques Offenbach, director of the Parisian theater Les Bouffes-Parisiens) that evolved out of the *opéra-comique* and later became the French opérette during the last years of the Second Empire. That period of transition—characterized by a spirit of easygoing skepticism, a reaction to the Voltaireanism of the preceding century—seemed to permeate society. Everything was approached with a light heart, possibly to hide any feelings of disquietude caused by the instability of the regime. After the war of 1870, the taste of the public appeared to undergo a change, and the opérette—which combined certain characteristics of the *opéra-bouffe* and of the older *opéra-comique*—came into vogue.

26. An exclusively French style of opera. The *opéra-comique* (comic opera) developed from earlier popular shows performed by troupes entertaining spectators at fairs. An *opéra-comique* consists of spoken dialogue alternating with musical numbers (arias and orchester). The theater named Opéra-Comique in Paris was founded in 1715. The repertoire of the *opéra-comique* contains works as well known as Mozart's *All Women Do So* (*Così Fan Tutte*, 1790), Donizetti's *The Daughter of the Regiment* (*La Fille du Régiment*, 1840), Berlioz's *The Trojans* (*Les Troyens*, 1856–1859), Bizet's *Carmen* (1875), Offenbach's *The Tales of Hoffmann* (*Les Contes d'Hoffmann*, 1880), Verdi's *Falstaff* (1893), and Debussy's *Pelléas et Melisande* (1902).

27. *Les Deux orphelines*, 1874. *The Two Orphans* premiered on stage in New York in 1875. Kate Claxton, the star who played Louise, made this role famous, and owned the American rights to the play. *The Two Orphans* was very popular with American audiences. The popularity of the play inspired at least one French and three American film adaptations. The French film version, *Les Deux orphelines* (1910) was directed by Albert Capellani. The first two American versions were filmed by the Selig Polyscope Company. The first version (1908) was a one-reeler lasting twelve to fifteen minutes. Little is known about this lost film. Selig's second adaptation (1911) was three reels

long, and directed by Otis Turner. It starred Kathlyn Williams as Henriette and Winnifred Greenwood as Louise. Both Selig versions were moderately successful. In 1915, Fox Film Corporation produced its version (still called *The Two Orphans*), directed by Herbert Brenon. It starred none other than Theda Bara as Henriette and Jean Sothern as Louise. This version received good reviews from critics, but failed at the box office. Unfortunately, this film does not exist today. *Orphans of the Storm* (United Artists, 1921), the last of D.W. Griffith's blockbuster epics, was produced with opulent sets, wonderful costumes, and attention to detail. This was also the last film collaboration of the great film director and his discoveries Lillian and Dorothy Gish. Both sisters left Griffith's company after ten years and joined Henry King's Inspiration Pictures. They would appear together again in *Romola* (Inspiration Pictures, for Metro-Goldwyn, 1925).

    28. *Kéraban-le-têtu* (Paris: Hetzel, 1883).

    29. *Mathias Sandorf* (Paris: Hetzel, 1885).

    30. "Maître Zacharius," *Musée des Familles* (April and May 1854): 193–200 and 225–31.

    31. The philosophy of Saint-Simonianism was created by Claude Henri de Rouvroy, Count of Saint-Simon (1760–1825), a French socialist born in Paris. At the age of sixteen he went to the United States to fight in the American Revolution. When he returned to France, he supported the Revolution there, giving up his title. He is considered one of the founders of modern socialism.

    32. *L'Ile mystérieuse* (Paris: Hetzel, 1874–1875).

    33. *Les Cinq cents millions de la Bégum* (Paris: Hetzel, 1879).

    34. Paschal Grousset (1845–1909), French science fiction novelist who wrote under the pseudonym of André Laurie and was published by Hetzel. His science fiction novels, known as *Les Romans d'aventures* (*The Adventure Novels*) and published between 1884 and 1905, truly comprise the first science fiction series ever published.

    35. *Maître du monde* (Paris: Hetzel, 1904).

    36. *Le Château des Carpathes* (Paris: Hetzel, 1892).

    37. *Face au drapeau* (Paris: Hetzel, 1896).

    38. "Le docteur Ox" (Paris: Hetzel, 1874).

    39. Jacques Offenbach (1819–1880), French composer whose operettas are considered masterpieces of the *opéra-comique*. He was born in Cologne, Germany, and studied at the Paris Conservatoire. By 1875 he had composed ninety operettas.

    40. *Voyage au centre de la terre* (Paris: Hetzel, 1864).

41. *Hector Servadac* (Paris: Hetzel, 1877).

42. Jules Barbier (1825–1901), French librettist who worked with Gounod and Offenbach.

43. Michel Carré (1819–1872), French librettist who worked with Offenbach and Jules Verne.

44. Parisian theater opened in 1782 and is still in use today.

45. Jules Verne began to work on *Mona Lisa* in 1851 and was still working on it in 1855, when he wrote a letter to his mother indicating that he was changing the title from *Leonardo da Vinci* to *Mona Lisa*. This play is in verse and was never produced on stage. Jules Verne read it publicly in 1874 at the Académie d'Amiens. Its first publication was in 1974, in the twenty-fifth issue of the magazine *Cahiers de l'Herne*. It's available in book form (Paris: L'Herne, 1995).

46. *Voyages et aventures du capitaine Hatteras* (Paris: Hetzel, 1866).

47. *Autour de la lune* (Paris: Hetzel, 1870).

48. *L'Ecole des robinsons* (Paris: Hetzel, 1882).

49. *Le Rayon vert* (Paris: Hetzel, 1882).

50. *Le Tour du monde en quatre-vingts jours* (Paris: Hetzel, 1873).

51. *L'Etoile du sud* (Paris: Hetzel, 1884).

52. *Sans dessus dessous* (Paris: Hetzel, 1889).

53. *Robur le Conquérant* (Paris: Hetzel, 1886).

54. *L'Ile à hélice* (Paris: Hetzel, 1895).

55. Jules Verne and Adolphe d'Ennery, *Voyage à travers l'Impossible* (Paris: J.-J. Pauvert, 1981). Introduction, notes, and comments by François Raymond and Robert Pourvoyeur.

56. Joseph Laissus, "Le Voyage à travers l'Impossible," *Bulletin de la Société Jules Verne* (Nouvelle série) 3, no. 12 (October–December 1969): 79–81.

57. Robert Pourvoyeur, "Du nouveau . . . sur l'Impossible!" *Bulletin de la Société Jules Verne* (Nouvelle série) 12, no. 45 (January–March 1978): 137–51.

58. Oscar-Louis-Antoine-Ferdinand de Lagoanère, French composer, born in Bordeaux on August 25, 1853. He was a prolific and successful composer and conductor. In the 1880s he became director of the Théâtre des Menus-Plaisirs and later of the Théâtre des Bouffes-Parisiens. His last known work was published in 1907. Nothing of him is known after that date.

NOTES TO THE PLAY

ACT 1: THE CENTER OF THE EARTH

1. Andernak is sometimes used for Andernach, a German town on the Rhine River between Koblenz and Bonn. A similar name is used by Jules Verne in the short story "Master Zacharius" (published by Hetzel in 1874) in which the castle of Andernatt is located somewhere in the Swiss Alps, where the real town of Andermatt exists. A music lover, Jules Verne was inspired by Jacques Offenbach; Andernak rhymes with the repetitive phrases in "*Va pour Kleinzach*," from act I, scene 6, of Offenbach's *The Tales of Hoffmann*, which was running in February 1881 at the Opéra-Comique in Paris. *Journey Through the Impossible* has the same structure as *The Tales of Hoffmann*. Jules Verne loved to play with words and was used to intertextual anagrams between his works (e.g., Arneka in *The School of Robinsons* and Artenak in *Mathias Sandorf*). There is a consanguinity between *Journey Through the Impossible* and *The School of Robinsons* (e.g., the character of Tartelet, the similarity between Andernak and Arneka, and between Kolderup and Finderup).

2. This musical instrument plays an important role in two Verne works: *Twenty Thousand Leagues under the Sea* and "Mr. D Sharp and Miss E Flat" ("Monsieur Ré-dièze et mademoiselle Mi-bémol," also known as "Mr. Ray Sharp and Miss Me Flat").

3. In 1885, in *Mathias Sandorf*, Verne has a character named Toronthal.

4. A novel published in 1866 by Hetzel with the title *Voyages et aventures du capitaine Hatteras* (*Journeys and Adventures of Captain Hatteras*, also known as *The English at the North Pole* and *The Field of Ice*). Captain John Hatteras remains obsessed by a strong idea: to plant the British flag at the North Pole. This hard, proud man has already organized two expeditions that ended tragically. So when he orders a new ship and hires a new crew, he takes care to remain anonymous. Richard Shandon and Dr. Clawbonny both receive letters signed with a single initial, inviting them to accompany an expedition on the high seas, destination unknown. As the chief officer, Shandon is empowered to assemble the crew and pay for construction of the ship for this adventure, the brig *Forward*, designed for navigation in the polar seas. The ship is quickly built, launched, receives its orders, and departs Liverpool, sailing north toward Melville Bay. Dr. Clawbonny, the ship's physician, is erudite with an alert curiosity, gaiety, and optimism. Even as the ship heads north, the captain has not made an appearance. Eventually a member of the crew reveals himself to be Captain John Hatteras. Recruited as a

simple sailor, Hatteras abruptly reveals his true identity and immediately gains Clawbonny's confidence. However, the other members of the crew have difficulty accepting the iron discipline imposed by the commander, as they realize the purpose of the voyage: for their British crew to be the first to reach the North Pole. In the polar winter, the brig is immobilized by ice and a necessary frigid dormancy is made even worse by the lack of fuel. A desperate expedition that is organized to discover a hypothetical deposit of coal unfortunately fails. While the expedition is away, Shandon leads the crew in a mutiny that destroys the ship. When returning, Hatteras and Clawbonny find the *Forward* burned; the crew has left, trying to find their way back to England. With two faithful sailors, Hatteras and Clawbonny find Captain Altamont, an American who also had to abandon his ship and who is desperately ill from starvation and exposure. After seventeen days of exhaustive walking, the five men succeed in finding the wreck of Altamont's ship, which provides them food, coal, and enough wood to build a launch. Soon Hatteras and Altamont fight violently, because the Englishman suspects the American of wanting to reach the pole and claim it for his country. However, they reconcile after a dramatic hunting party during which Altamont saves Hatteras's life. In the spring, the launch is lodged onto a large sled, driven to the edge of free water, and put to sea. After a few days of navigation, the explorers land on a steep island: the North Pole is there, atop an active volcano. Under the influence of "polar madness," Hatteras climbs the sides of the volcano, unfurls the flag, and slips into the crater. Caught up at the last second by Altamont, he remains dazed and his companions understand that he has lost his reason. Ice blocks their route south, so the travelers abandon the boat and continue by foot to the Baffin Sea. Exhausted and without resources, they are finally saved by a whaling ship and returned to England. Hatteras lives out his life in a mental institution, enclosed in his insanity, not recognizing his friends, having forgotten everything, except the direction north, the invariable direction he takes when he walks.

In Verne's first version of the book, which was never published, Hatteras fell in the volcano and died at the North Pole. However, because Verne's marketplace was the educated French family (able to read and write), Hetzel believed such a conclusion might shock young readers, so he asked Verne to revise the end of the novel. Verne did so, but with an artistic and solemn pirouette, leaving Hatteras afflicted by polar madness, walking always north. A hundred years after the discovery of the North Pole by Captain Hatteras, the Collège de Pataphysique in Paris celebrated this anniversary with a huge banquet and many speeches. Members of the Collège de Pataphysique

included Boris Vian, Eugen Ionesco, Paul-Emile Victor, and Raymond Que-
neau (see Viridis Candela, *Cahiers acénonètes du Collège de Pataphysique*, no. 16
(July 11, 1961).

5. One of the two comical characters of the play. In *The School of Robinsons*, published in 1882 by Hetzel, the dance master is named T. Artelett. The
connection is obvious.

6. Written "Lidenbrock" in *Journey to the Center of the Earth* (*Voyage au
center de la terre*), published in 1864 by Hetzel in Paris. This geology novel
of Jules Verne begins in Hamburg, in 1863, where an eminent mineralogist,
Professor Otto Lidenbrock, discovers a cryptographic manuscript hidden in
an old Icelandic book. Not without sorrow, and with the help of his nephew
Axel, he manages to decipher it. The short note—written by Saknussemm,
an alchemist of the sixteenth century—shows the way to the center of the
earth. In spite of the reservations of the peaceful Axel, snatched from his
comfort and from his fiancée, the professor decides at once to follow the
traces of the traveler who tried the adventure three hundred years before.
The "entry door" indicated by the parchment is Snaeffels (in Icelandic, Snae-
fellsjökull), an extinct volcano in Iceland. Accompanied by Hans, their Icelandic guide, the two men go down in one of the eruptive chimneys and
begin their underground progression by the glow from the Ruhmkorff
lamps. The entrails of the globe reveal fairy-like visions, and the advance of
the explorers is slowed down by dramatic incidents. First a lack of water
makes them suffer cruelly, until Hans discovers a providential creek; then
Axel is lost in the total darkness of a granite labyrinth and loses consciousness, after having fallen down the slope of a "vertical gallery, a veritable well"
(William Butcher's translation). Found by his companions, he awakes in a
cave of gigantic dimensions; the ceiling rises as far as the eye can see, and the
cave contains an entire sea. In this sea and on its shores, the flora and fauna
of an ancient geological time still remain, to the great amazement of the professor. The crossing of the sea on a raft is disturbed by a fight between an
ichthyosaurus and a plesiosaurus, and by an appalling storm. On the other
side, the travelers find a sign left by Saknussemm. The way is blocked, and
they use explosives to open a passage, which turns out to be a catastrophic
initiative. The raft is lifted by a tidal wave into a volcanic chimney and
pushed to the surface of the earth by the molten magma. At the end of a dis-
tressing rise, the three men, bruised but safe, find themselves on the slopes
of Stromboli, a volcano in full eruption. From Iceland to the Eolian Islands,
they traverse twenty-four hundred miles and live a fabulous Plutonian adventure. Professor Lidenbrock becomes world-famous, but regrets not having

been able to reach the center of the earth. Axel is finally able to marry his betrothed.

7. Latin word meaning "nobody" or "no man" (in Homer's *Odyssey*, Odysseus declares his name to be "Noman," when he encounters the Cyclops Polyphemus). Nemo is used by Jules Verne as the name of the captain of the *Nautilus* in *Twenty Thousand Leagues under the Sea* and *Mysterious Island*. The first novel begins in 1867, in New York. The French professor Aronnax embarks on board a frigate of the American navy, with the objective to hunt and destroy the giant narwhal whose aggressiveness toward ships concerns ship owners. After a long journey, the frigate approaches the monster, but the encounter turns bad and, during the short confrontation that follows, the scientist is thrown into the sea with his servant Conseil and the harpooner Ned Land. The three climb on the back of the narwhal and quickly note that it is not an animal, but an enormous steel machine. Taken aboard, they are greeted by the enigmatic Captain Nemo who designed and built this extraordinary submarine, the *Nautilus*. This man, whose nationality and identity remain unknown, seems to harbor violent hatred for a country that is never identified in the novel. The involuntary guests of the captain cannot be released because they now know the secret of the *Nautilus*. Aronnax deals well with the detention, because it allows him to satisfy his passion for ichthiology under exceptional conditions. The port-holes of the *Nautilus* reveal to him the wonders of the Atlantic and Pacific Oceans. During a tour of the underwater world, he feels the emotions of underwater explorers, visits the fisheries of Ceylon, and contemplates the ruins of Atlantis. He also lives dramatic moments during the crossing of the ice-barrier of the South Pole, where the ship escapes being crushed by ice. With Ned Land, he fights against the giant octopuses that attack the crew and the ship, and admires the bravery of Nemo on this occasion. In spite of the sympathy he feels for this exceptional man, the scientist is indignant when the *Nautilus* rams and pitilessly sinks a warship. Pushed by Conseil and Ned Land, Aronnax agrees to try to escape. When the *Nautilus* is sucked down in the Maëlström, the three escape in a dinghy and avoid the deadly pressure of the flow. They are rescued by Norwegian fishermen, but the *Nautilus* is not seen again. Did Nemo succumb? Will his true name and his nationality remain unknown? These questions remain unanswered for Aronnax.

According to Adolphe Brisson, who visited Jules Verne in 1898, and on Verne's own confession, the idea of an underwater voyage was suggested to him by the novelist George Sand, an assiduous reader of his novels. Brisson published Sand's letter *in extenso* in his interview. Paul Verne, brother of the novelist and captain in the merchant marine, was consulted for the technical questions about the *Nautilus*. In 1874, Jules Verne reintroduced the character of Nemo in *Mysterious Island* and provided his true identity and his biography. Verne had initially created Nemo as a Polish prince fighting against Russia. Hetzel asked him to modify Nemo's nationality for commercial and political reasons: France was an ally of Russia and Verne's translations in Russian were a good market. Verne accommodated his publisher by making Nemo an Indian prince fighting against the British.

In *Twenty Thousand Leagues under the Sea*, Nemo is in his forties; in *Mysterious Island*, he is seventy, even though the first novel happens in 1866 and the second in 1869. In writing *Twenty Thousand Leagues under the Sea*, Verne knew he would have to bring Nemo back in a later novel, to unveil his nationality and identity. He planned to do it when Nemo would be seventy, but Hetzel asked him to put Nemo in another novel much earlier than he had planned. Hence Nemo's appearance in *Mysterious Island*. Verne and Hetzel both knew the problem this would cause but they didn't correct it. They merely placed two footnotes in *Mysterious Island* making the reader aware of their decision to leave the dates as they were.

8. Michel Ardan is one of the three passengers of the bullet going *From the Earth to the Moon*. In Verne's novel, he comes from France just in time to ask the Gun Club to modify the projectile, saying in his telegram, "Modify it, I will travel inside." Ardan is also the anagram of Nadar, alias Félix Tournachon, photographer and balloonist friend of Jules Verne.

9. Aalborg, a city in northern Denmark (www.aalborg.dk), contains the world's largest Viking burial ground, a cathedral, a monastery, large Renaissance buildings, and a castle. The Andernak Castle, is based on the castle in Aalborg. During the spring of 1881, Jules Verne traveled from Rotterdam to Copenhagen on his yacht, *Saint-Michel III*, with a crew of ten mariners. With him was his brother Paul, who wrote a report of this journey under the title *De Rotterdam à Copenhague à bord du yacht Saint-Michel*. Hetzel added the report to the end of the in-octavo edition of the novel *The Jangada* (*La Jangada*, also known as *Eight Hundred Leagues over the Amazon*). Was it this trip that inspired Jules Verne to set the beginning of *Journey Through the Impossible* in Denmark? In a letter to Hetzel, written from Rotterdam on June 8, 1881, Jules Verne cites the town of Frederickshaven, north of Aalborg Bay, on the Kattegat, a gulf of the North Sea bounded by Norway, Denmark, and Sweden.

10. In 1872, Verne published a short story titled "An Imagination of Dr. Ox," serialized in three issues of *Le Musée des Familles*. The small town of Quiquendone is wisely managed by the burgomaster Van Tricasse and his

friend and adviser Niklausse. The Quiquendonians are phlegmatic and placid people, living in a perpetual slowdown. But everything changes with the arrival of the vibrant Dr. Ox, who offers to install gas lighting throughout the town, at no charge, with the agreement of the burgomaster. A plant is built, the gas pipes are run under the pavement, and the standard lamps grow like mushrooms in the streets. What is the true objective of Dr. Ox and his assistant, Ygène? The personality and the character of the Quiquendonians change drastically: they become speedy and aggressive. Van Tricasse and Niklausse start a violent fight, compromising the wedding of their children. The town declares war on the neighboring town over a minor litigation several centuries old. A drama seems imminent at the time the whole population attacks the supposed enemy, when an enormous explosion destroys the gas plant. The excitement disappears as the Quiquendonians, calm again, walk peacefully back home. The reader learns that all the upset was caused by Dr. Ox, an eminent physiologist who circulated pure oxygen in public places to observe the effects on the inhabitants. Quiquendone is left without lighting, but once again has peace and quiet after the headlong escape of the scientist and his assistant. Verne jokes with words: Ox plus Ygène makes oxygen. The story inspired an *opera-bouffe* in 1877 with a libretto by Philippe Gille and music by Jacques Offenbach.

11. Verne's (or Nemo's?) submarine was named after the *Nautilus* of Robert Fulton, the American inventor of the steam engine. In 1800, Robert Fulton (1765–1815) presented to the French Directoire a submarine to sink British ships. During the demonstration in Rouen, on the river Seine, Fulton himself was aboard and his *Nautilus* dove to a depth of 7.6 meters (25 feet).

12. In Greek mythology, the Titans ruled the universe for ages. They were massive and strong, and were the twelve children of Uranus (heaven) and Gaea (Earth). The best known are Chronos (Time), who ruled the universe until he was dethroned by his son Zeus; Oceanos was the river flowing around the earth. Oceanos's wife, Tethys, was the goddess of the Mediterranean Sea. Mnemosyne was the goddess of memory and the mother of the nine Muses. Themis was the goddess of divine justice, and Atlas, of course, carried the world on his shoulders.

13. A volcano close to Naples.

14. Italian town at the foot of the volcano Vesuvius. Lidenbrock and his two companions came out of their *Journey to the Center of the Earth* through Stromboli, not through Vesuvius. Parisian spectators were more familiar with Naples and Vesuvius than with Stromboli.

15. A suburb northwest of Paris, on the river Seine.

16. There is no such place as Asnières de Bigorre. But in the Pyrenees

(a mountain range between France and Spain), above Tarbes, on the Adour River, is a resort called Bagnières de Bigorre.

17. In *Journey to the Center of the Earth*, Axel was professor Lidenbrock's nephew who traveled with him and the Icelandic guide Hans underground from the Snaeffels to the Stromboli.

18. Jules Verne loved to play with names and words. He invented Babichok to be hilarious and ridiculous. Valdemar's fiancée had to have a name that would add comical effects.

19. Verne plays here with the French word "battement," which has a double meaning: tapping or stamping and palpitation. Tartelet uses it with the first meaning, while Valdemar uses it with the second, thus creating a misunderstanding that is always well received on stage.

20. Untranslatable (double meaning) wordplay: In French, "Suisse" is both a noun and an adjective. In English, we have Switzerland and Swiss, two different words. In French, the adjective is placed after the noun, so Tartelet could understand Valdemar saying ". . . mouton. Suisse . . ." as "Swiss mutton" when Valdemar wanted to say: ". . . mutton. Switzerland . . ."

21. Another example of Verne's play with words. This name is as comical and ridiculous as Babichok. In the novel serialized by Hetzel in 1882, when *Journey Through the Impossible* was on stage in Paris, *The School of Robinsons* (*L'école des Robinsons*) is a character named William W. Kolderup.

22. Verne's expression "carrefour des écrasés" means literally the "intersection of the crushed." Of course, there is no such place in Paris, or anywhere, and the use of the term adds to the comical aspect of the dialogue. Valdemar means "the crossroads where many people were run over."

23. After successfully publishing four novels by Jules Verne, Hetzel decided to give them a generic title: *Extraordinary Journeys*. Verne's novels were extraordinary adventures, but this play *makes them impossible. Journey Through the Impossible* is, with its summary, the crown of the collection of *Extraordinary Journeys*.

24. At the beginning of his literary career, Jules Verne wrote *Journey to the Center of the Earth* and touched on the topic of evolution. Later he deepened the subject in *The Aerial Village*, where the members of a safari in the Congo discover what appears to be a colony of natives living in the trees.

25. One of the four basic forces of nature: fire, water, air, and earth. Later, in *Master of the World* (*Maître du monde*), Verne imagines an automobile capable of traveling on Earth, an aircraft to fly, and a submarine to navigate on and under water. The "Terror" (L'Epouvante) will be destroyed by the fourth element, fire, in its most symbolic aspect—lightning.

26. There are three ballets in the play, according to the reviews, one at the end of every act. The text doesn't mention the second ballet.

ACT II: THE BOTTOM OF THE SEA

1. A district on the west coast of India, colonized by Afonso de Albuquerque in 1510. Goa remained a Portuguese colony until 1962, when it became part of India. Why did Jules Verne choose to begin the underwater part of *Journey Through the Impossible* in Goa? According to Charles-Noël Martin, it's because of Oscar de Lagoanère, the composer and director of the music in *Journey Through the Impossible*. His name contains the letters "goa"—another Vernean wordplay. Robert Pourvoyeur suggests two other interpretations: one, Nemo, the captain of the *Nautilus*, was Indian, and Goa is close to his homeland (in 1882, it was still a Portuguese colony). Second, Goa is wordplay: in French, a jeweler is "un joailler" and a banterer is "un gouailleur." Verne could have planned to use Goa as part of a combination of these two words that are almost homonyms. He didn't use the joke in the play, but it was used by Arnold Mortier in his review of the play, which can be found at the end of this volume.

2. A common British and American family name, but also the name of Sir James Anderson who commanded the *Great Eastern* from Liverpool to New York and back in April 1862, with Jules Verne and his brother Paul on board. His one and only trip to America gave Jules Verne the opportunity to write his most autobiographic novel *A Floating City* (*Une Ville flottante*)—with parts of fiction—in which he describes the ship, the captain, some passengers, and his visit to Niagara Falls. Anderson is also the name of the captain of the *Scotia*, the ship rammed by the *Nautilus* in the first chapter of *Twenty Thousand Leagues under the Sea*.

3. A Venetian gold ducat (coin with the ruling doge's portrait on it) created at the end of the thirteenth century. The sequin became the common business coin around the Mediterranean and was imitated all over Europe.

4. "This proved that this extraordinary cetacean could transport itself from one place to another with amazing speed" (*Twenty Thousand Leagues under the Sea*, chapter 1).

5. A major seaport and manufacturing center in central Chile, on a wide bay of the Pacific Ocean. It's one of Chile's largest cities. Because of the sonority of the word, Valparaiso is part of many French popular songs and mariner's songs.

6. The battle against the giant squid is one of the most powerful scenes

of *Twenty Thousand Leagues under the Sea*. It is no surprise that before Walt Disney used it in 1954, Verne himself used it again in *Journey Through the Impossible*.

7. A word often used by Verne in *Twenty Thousand Leagues under the Sea*, as a synonym for squid or octopus. Kraken, a word of Norwegian origin, was already in use in the middle of the eighteenth century, and meant a fabulous sea monster.

8. Verne (or d'Ennery?) invented the name of a ship whose sonority would get across on stage. There was such ship sunk in *Twenty Thousand Leagues Under the Sea*. *Tranquebar* is also the contraction of "tranquil" and "bar."

9. According to many biographers, Jules Verne often said, "I love three things more than everything else: music, the sea, and liberty."

10. Charles-Noël Martin credits Verne with this sentence, which comments about the atheist orientation taken in 1877 by the "Grand Orient de France" (the highest Masonic lodge in France).

11. In *Mysterious Island*, the last words of Captain Nemo are "God and Fatherland," which is surprising in the mouth of an anarchist, the independent captain of *Twenty Thousand Leagues under the Sea*. Verne was asked by Hetzel to modify Nemo's last words in deference to the French family, to be "bourgoise" and "politically correct." Verne and d'Ennery show here the very devout side of Nemo.

12. Reference to the end of *Journeys and Adventures of Captain Hatteras*—in the first Verne manuscript (never published)—in which Hatteras dies falling into the volcano at the North Pole. This shows Verne reacting to his publisher, Hetzel, who obliged him to modify the end of *Hatteras* and save the captain, and, in whose opinion *Journey Through the Impossible* was an insane undertaking.

13. The oyster described here by Valdemar is the same as the one shown by Nemo to professor Aronnax in *Twenty Thousand Leagues under the Sea*, housing a gigantic pearl that grew from an impurity deposited by Nemo. *Tridacna gigas* is the world's largest bivalve. A true giant, this species of oyster can reach lengths of over four feet, and can weigh over five hundred pounds. The species is generally found on a substratum of coral reef, and lives in depths from only a few feet to several fathoms. It can be found from the Philippines to Micronesia. A photograph of it can be seen at: www.oncampus.richmond.edu/cultural/museums/lrginfo/25/24giant_clam.html.

14. Here is another example of Verne playing with words. In French, the expression "plancher des vaches" (literally "floor of the cows") means "land" or "dry land" and is used by someone who spends little time on dry land.

Valdemar uses the expression "veal's floor" ("plancher des veaux") meaning dry land or just land in Copenhagen. Tartelet corrects him immediately, explaining that in France, the expression is "the floor of their mothers."

15. This noted Greek philosopher wrote about Atlantis in two of his dialogues, the *Timaeus* and the *Critias*, around 370 B.C.E.

16. One of the cities of Atlantis, according to Jules Verne in *Twenty Thousand Leagues under the Sea*. Makhimos is not mentioned in Plato's *Critias* (the origin of all legends about Atlantis).

17. Mentioned by Plutarch in his life of Sertorius. Around 80 B.C.E., a roman general, Sertorius, former governor of Spain, goes to Mauretania (today's Morocco) with his army and conquers Tingis (today's Tangier), whose king, Ascalis, might otherwise come back from exile to reclaim his throne. In 38 B.C.E. Octavius (who became Emperor Augustus) gave Tingis the status of Roman Colony.

18. The ancient Egyptian deity whose name means "hidden." Amon or Ammon, the god of reproductive forces, was part of the divine triad of Thebes, with his wife, Mut, and his son Khon. Later Amon was identified with the sun god Ra, and was called Amon-Ra, the father of the gods and the creator all living beings. As such, he became identified with Zeus in ancient Greek, and with Jupiter in Rome. In the play, the use of Ammon connects Atlantis with ancient Egypt.

19. In Greek mythology, demigod Atlas was punished by Zeus and condemned to bear the sky (with the earth) forever on his back. In classical architecture, *atlantes* (the plural form of *atlas*) are male figures used as columns to support a superstructure. Atlantes are the male counterpart of caryatids and could also be the inhabitants of Atlantis. Verne logically named their king Atlas.

20. A name made up by Verne. In classical Greek, Selene means Moon.

21. In Greek mythology, Electra was the daughter of Agamemnon (the winner of the Trojan War and hero of Homer's *Iliad*) and Clytemnestra. During the Trojan War, Clytemnestra had an affair with Egisthe and they killed Agamemnon as he came home after the war. To avenge her father's death, Electra pushed her brother Orestes to kill Egisthe and Clytemnestra. What a family! Over the centuries, Electra's vengeance has inspired Eschylus (*The Choephores*, 458 B.C.E.), Sophocles (415 B.C.E.), Euripides (413 B.C.E.), Eugene O'Neill (*Mourning Becomes Electra*, 1931), and Jean Giraudoux (*Électre*, 1937).

22. In Greek and Roman mythology a sibyl is a female fortune-teller inspired with prophetic power by Apollo. Sibyls lived in caves and prophesied in a frenzied trance, sitting on tripods.

ACT III: THE PLANET ALTOR

1. Verne described the president of the Gun Club as follows: "Impey Barbicane was a man of forty, calm, cold, austere, eminently serious and self-contained; punctual as a chronometer; in temperament, ready for any ordeal; in character, unshakable; adventurous but not romantic; always bringing practical ideas to bear on the boldest ventures; the ultimate New Englander, the colonizing Northerner; the descendant of the Roundheads, who were so deadly for the Stuarts; indeed the implacable foe of all Cavaliers, whether royalists in the Old Country or Southern gentlemen in the new. In short, a Yankee through and through" (*From the Earth to the Moon*, updated edition by Walter James Miller, 1995).

2. As the secretary of the Gun Club, Maston was present in all novels of the Gun Club Trilogy: *From the Earth to the Moon* (*De la terre à la lune*), *Around the Moon* (*Autour de la lune*), and *Topsy-Turvy* (*Sans dessus dessous*, also translated into English as *The Purchase of the North Pole*).

3. A type of heavy cast-iron cannon or howitzer used in the U.S. Army in the middle of the nineteenth century and during the Civil War. The Columbiad is a kind of Dahlgren that is, a piece of ordnance thick in the breech, and tapering off gradually from the base to the muzzle. See photos at www.fpc.dos.state.fl.us/learning/CivilWar/photos/Columbiad.html.

4. Stoney Hill, southeast of Tampa, is the location where the giant Columbiad was built to send the three Verne astronauts *From the Earth to the Moon* in 1864.

5. Captain Nicholl is, with Impey Barbicane and Michel Ardan, one of the three astronauts who travel *From the Earth to the Moon* (1865) and *Around the Moon* (1869). In *Topsy-Turvy* (1889), Nicholl invents the meli-melonite, a powerful explosive used to straighten Earth's axis.

6. Almost the same wording as in the letter Barbicane sends to all Gun Club members at the beginning of *From the Earth to the Moon*, inviting them to the meeting where the Gun Club decides to launch a bullet to the Moon.

7. The Phoenician and Chaldean goddess of fertility and love, also known as Isthar in ancient Assyria and Babylonia. She has been identified with various Greek goddesses: Selene, the goddess of the Moon (to whom Jules Verne dedicated an entire chapter in his Moon novels); Artemis, the goddess of hunting, twin sister of Apollo, and, Aphrodite, the goddess of love and beauty.

8. In ancient Greek mythology, he was the son of Zeus and Leto. Apollo was the god of the Sun, thus the adjective "radiant," as used by Jules

Verne. Apollo was also the god of music, poetry, and the arts. He is one of the most complex gods of the Greek pantheon. His twin sister, Artemis, was the goddess of the Moon and of hunting.

9. Two suburbs west of Paris, north of Versailles, on the river Seine. In the second half of the nineteenth century, Chatou and its neighbor Le Vésinet were popular for Sunday excursions by Parisians. These towns offered cafés, restaurants, and boats for rent. Chatou and Le Vésinet were favorite places of the impressionist painters. Renoir stayed in Chatou in 1879.

10. Reference to the Harvard College Observatory, founded in Cambridge, Massachusetts, in 1839, and reestablished from 1843 to 1847 by public subscription. In *From the Earth to the Moon* and *Around the Moon*, Verne writes of the "Cambridge Observatory" and of J.-M. Belfast, its director, who was supportive of the Gun Club project to send a bullet to the Moon.

11. The Columbiad of *From the Earth to the Moon* was completely underground, with its opening at ground level, but imagining the giant cannon on a stand is much more spectacular.

12. The legend of the Aymon Knights begins with the Emperor Charlemagne who knighted the four Aymon brothers. Yet Charlemagne lived to regret this act of generosity when Raynaud (or Renaud), the eldest of the Aymon Knights, killed Charlemagne's favorite nephew in an act of family honor. While on a run to the hillside of Dinant (Belgium), the four Aymon brothers—Raynaud, Alard, Guichard, and Richard—were suddenly surprised by Charlemagne's troops. They were completely surrounded with nowhere to turn when something extraordinary happened: Bayard, their mighty steed, leaped from the cliffs with all four knights on his back and landed safely on the other side of the Meuse River and galloped through the Ardennes. Thus they escaped the vengeance of the emperor. Outside of the city of Dinant is a rock, *le rocher Bayard* (the Bayard rock), which stands separate from the rest of the main rock to which it was once connected. The Bayard rock was detached with an explosion to provide passage for the French troops of Louis XIV after they took Dinant. However, popular belief has it that the rock was split by the hoof of their giant horse, Bayard, when it jumped over the Meuse River.

13. The French expression is "wagon projectile," which means literally "carriage projectile" or "coach missile."

14. A bitter yellow compound obtained by nitrating phenol. It is used as a dye and in the manufacture of explosives.

15. One of the bridges of Paris that span the river Seine, connecting the Place de la Concorde with the Assemblée Nationale (French Congress).

16. Valdemar jokes about the French National Assembly, which is called "Chambre des Députés." The expression means the building and the Assembly of elected representatives of France.

17. Verne's political ideas were mainly studied by the leftist university professor Jean Chesneaux, whose book was translated into English in 1972 (*The Political and Social Ideas of Jules Verne.* Translated by Thomas Wikeley [London: Thames and Hudson]). An important part of Chesneaux's view was based on Verne's *The Castaways of the Jonathan* (published by Hetzel in 1910), which is an apology for anarchism. Vernian scholars have since discovered that the novel was rewritten and transformed by Michel Verne, Jules's son, before the 1910 publication. The original text, written only by Jules Verne between October 17, 1897, and April 11, 1898, is available in English (*Magellania* [New York: Welcome Rain Publishers, 2002]) and shows much more moderate political views than Michel's rewriting. Jean Chesneaux also modified his book (only in French, *Jules Verne, un regard sur le monde* [Paris: Bayard, 2001]) to adapt his opinions to what Jules Verne wrote himself, without any external text manipulation. It's interesting to note that Valdemar promotes a society without government sixteen years before the novelist wrote his novel.

18. Verne was always in favor of what is today called the environment. Without being a "green environmentalist" (the concept didn't exist at his time), he envisioned that the mining of energy sources would impoverish the earth. In *A Floating City* (chap. 39), he writes: "Here we had a last view of the magnificent Niagara cataract. Our companion observed it with a thoughtful air.

" 'Isn't it grand, sir? Isn't it magnificent?' I said to him.

" 'Yes,' he replied; 'but what a waste of mechanical force, and what a mill might be turned with a fall as that!'

"Never did I feel more inclined to pitch an engineer into the water!"

19. The dialogue between Volsius and Ox confirms Verne's doubts about science and religion in the middle of his life (he was fifty-four in 1882). Volsius, spokesman of Verne, makes the first step toward Ox and asks him to use his science in a positive way. Ox and Volsius, the doctor and the priest, save George Hatteras from insanity and bring the play to a happy end.

APPENDIX

NOTES TO THE ARNOLD MORTIER REVIEW

1. A theater built in Paris, on the boulevard St-Martin, in 1781. Still in use today.

2. Adolphe Philippe (1811–1899), French playwright who used the pseudonyms of Dennery and d'Ennery. He wrote melodramas and opera libretti. His best-known work is *The Two Orphans* (*Les deux orphelines*). His wife's collection of oriental art belongs to the French nation and can still be seen today in the Musée d'Ennery in Paris.

3. Pseudonym of Paul Collin (1840–1906), director of the Théâtre de la Porte St-Martin 1879–1883.

4. Paul-Félix Taillade (1826–1898), French actor, who also performed in *The Children of Captain Grant* (*Les Enfants du capitaine Grant*).

5. Théâtre de l'Ambigu, one of the best-known theaters in Paris in the nineteenth century.

6. Joseph-François Dailly (1839–1897), French actor who created the role of Passepartout in *Around the World in Eighty Days* and plays Valdemar in *Journey Through the Impossible*.

7. A park in Paris. In December 1769 the Duke of Chartres bought a parcel of land a little more than one hectare (2.5 acres), which was the starting point of the future Monceau Park. He then increased the area by twelve hectares, to create a place for festivals and recreation. The park changed owners during the Revolution and the Restoration, and in 1860 became the property of the city of Paris, preserving half of its area as of that time. Its current configuration was inaugurated in August 1861 by Napoleon III.

8. Born in Bordeaux in 1853, Oscar-Louis-Antoine-Ferdinand de Lagoanère was a prolific and successful composer and conductor. In the 1880s he became director of the Théâtre des Menus-Plaisirs and later of the Théâtre des Bouffes-Parisiens. His last known work was published in 1907. Nothing is known about him after that date.

9. Auguste Rubé (1815–1899).

10. Philippe-Marie Chaperon (1823–1907).

11. A play on the French word "joailleur" (jeweller) and the city of Goa in India.

12. François René de Chateaubriand was a French writer born in Saint-Malo in 1786. He died in Paris in 1848.

13. French port on the Atlantic coast of Brittany. Its 50,000 inhabitants are known as "Malouins." During the fifteenth, seventeenth, and eighteenth centuries Saint-Malo was the home town of many seamen and corsairs. Chateaubriand's best-known portrait depicts him sitting on a rock in Saint-Malo, facing the Atlantic Ocean. Arnold Mortier uses this well-known icon to convey his impression of Taillade, as Doctor Ox, standing on the *Nautilus*, which looks to him like a rock.

14. Pseudonym of Gaspard-Félix Tournachon (April 5, 1820–March 21, 1910), a French writer, caricaturist, and photographer who is remembered primarily for his photographic portraits, which are considered to be among the best from the nineteenth century. He was one of Jules Verne's best friends.

15. A cathedral in Paris. A gothic masterpiece, Notre-Dame de Paris was conceived by Maurice de Sully and built between the twelfth and fourteenth centuries (1163–1345). Road distances in France are calculated on the basis of the "0 km" marked on the square in front of the cathedral.

NOTES TO THE
NEW YORK TIMES REVIEW

1. Written Eva in the play. The role was played by the French actress Marie Daubrun (1828–1901), who appeared on stage for the last time in 1889. Marie Daubrun was Baudelaire's mistress and inspired several of his poems.

2. An opera by Charles Gounod (1818–1893), performed in the Opera of Paris, April 1, 1881.

3. A French actor born in 1814, Augustin-Guillemet Alexandre also played in *Around the World in Eighty Days* and Tartelet in *Journey Through the Impossible*.

4. The unknown reviewer is confusing Sweden and Denmark. In the play, Valdemar is a Dane.

5. An opera by Georges Bizet (1838–1875), performed in the Opéra-Comique in Paris, March 3, 1875.

6. Pauline Patry, a French actress whose true name was Jeanne Cécile Pauline Pesty, began her career in 1873. She died in 1910.